THE
GOLD-RIMMED SPECTACLES

GIORGIO BASSANI

THE

GOLD-RIMMED

SPECTACLES

TRANSLATED FROM THE ITALIAN
BY ISABEL QUIGLY

NEW YORK ATHENEUM PUBLISHERS

1960

Copyright © 1960 by Atheneum House, Inc., and Faber and
Faber Limited; originally published in Italian under the title
GLI OCCHIALI D'ORO © 1958 by Giulio Einaudi Editore,
S. p. A., Turin. All rights reserved. Library of Congress catalog
card number 60–11035. Printed in the United States of America
by The Murray Printing Company, Forge Village,
Massachusetts; bound by H. Wolff, New York.
FIRST AMERICAN EDITION

THE

GOLD-RIMMED SPECTACLES

1

Time has begun to diminish—though there are still quite a few, at Ferrara—the number of those who remember Dr. Fadigati: Athos Fadigati, the ear, nose and throat specialist who lived and had his surgery in Via Gorgadello, near Piazza delle Erbe, and came to such a tragic end, poor fellow; and who, when he came from his home in Venice to settle here, seemed destined for the quietest, the most normal, and for that very reason the most enviable, of careers.

It was in 1919, just after the first world war. Because of my age, I can give only a rather vague, confused picture of how things were at the time. The cafés in the middle of town were crammed with officers in uniform; every minute, along Corso Giovecca and Corso Roma (renamed Corso Martyrs of Liberty some years ago) lorries went past with red flags waving; on the scaffolding that covered the front of the General Insurance building which was then going up opposite the north side of the Castle, hung an enormous advertisement on scarlet cloth, inviting friends and enemies of socialism to drink a LENIN APERITIF; fights between peasants and workmen armed with slogans on the one hand, and ex-servicemen on the other, broke out almost daily ... The feverish, agitated climate of general unrest, in which those of us who were to grow up in the next two decades spent our first years, must somehow have favoured the Venetian Fadigati. In a town like ours, where after the war young men of good family were more reluctant than anywhere else to return to the liberal professions, it was obviously easy for him to settle in almost without attracting attention. By 1925, when the rigours of those post-war years were beginning to lessen, and fascism, organized into a great national party, was in a position to offer improved conditions to all ex-servicemen, Athos Fadigati was already solidly installed in Ferrara, with a first-class private practice and, besides, was head of the ear, nose and throat department of the new Hospital of Sant'Anna.

He had, as they say, arrived. He was no longer very young, and already had an air of never having been so; and it appears he had left Venice (he said so himself once) not so much to seek his fortune in another city, as to get away from the painful atmosphere of an enormous house on the Grand Canal, where, in the space of a few years, he had seen die both his parents and a sister he loved dearly. People liked his politeness, his discretion, his obvious disinterestedness, his unobtrusive charity to the poorest of his patients. But the way he was made—physically, I mean—must have done even more to recommend him: the gold-rimmed spectacles that sparkled agreeably on his brownish, smooth cheeks, the not unpleasing stoutness of his big body, obviously that of a man with congenital heart-trouble who had miraculously come through the dangers of adolescence and was always wrapped up, even in summer, in soft English wool (his only war service had been, on account of his health, in censorship of the post). There was definitely something attractive and reassuring about him, right from the start.

His consulting room in Via Gorgadello, where he saw patients from four till seven every afternoon, later completed his success.

It was a really modern consulting room, the kind no doctor in Ferrara had ever possessed before. There was a spotless surgery that, for cleanliness, efficiency, and even size, could only be compared with those at Sant'Anna, and, besides that, no less than eight rooms of his private flat alongside were used as waiting rooms for the patients. The townsfolk, especially the socially prominent townsfolk, were dazzled. They were accustomed to the picturesque but huddled and unhealthy disorder in which the three or four established local doctors continued to receive their respective patients, and Fadigati's surgery touched them as if it denoted his personal appreciation of their value. When at Fadigati's, they never tired of repeating, did you have to wait interminably jumbled together like cattle, listening through the thin walls to the gay, rowdy voices of the doctor's family, while, in the dim light of a twenty-watt bulb, there was nothing to see on the gloomy walls but a majolica notice saying: DO NOT SPIT! or caricatures of teachers at the university or of colleagues, not to mention even grislier and more ghoulish pictures of patients having frightful injections before an entire medical school, or of operations in which death peeped grinning out of the surgeon's robes? And how, how on earth had they ever managed to put up with such medieval treatment till now?

A visit to Fadigati's soon became, not just the fashion, but an actual pleasure, an event. On winter evenings, when the freezing wind whistled down from Piazza del Duomo into Via Gorgadello, it was with real satisfaction that the rich citizen, bundled up in his great fur overcoat, made the tiniest sore throat an excuse to push open the half-open door at the corner of Via Bersaglieri del Po, climb two flights of stairs, and ring the bell at Fadigati's glass front door. Up there, beyond that magical luminous square, which was opened by a nurse in a white over-all—always young, always smiling—he found the central heating going full blast, not only better than in his own home but almost better than at the Merchants' Club or the Concordi; he found plenty of armchairs and sofas, plenty of small tables piled up with the latest magazines, shaded lights turned on in a generous, absolutely unstinted way; carpets that, when he tired of dozing in the warmth or flicking through the illustrated papers, made him wander from room to room looking at the numerous pictures and prints, old and modern, that hung on the walls. And at the end of it he found a cheerful, conversational doctor, who, while he took him personally in "beyond" to have a look at his throat, seemed above all anxious to know, like the real gentleman and passionate Wagnerian he was, if his patient had had a chance of hearing Aureliano Pertile in *Lohengrin* at Bologna a few evenings before; or else, say, if he had seen, on such and such a wall in such and such a room, a particular De Chirico or "Casoratino", or if he liked some particular De Pisis; and was really startled if, at the last question, his patient confessed not only that he didn't know the paintings of De Pisis, but that until now he had never heard that Filippo De Pisis was a promising young painter from Ferrara. A comfortable, agreeable, gentlemanly, even instructive atmosphere, in short, where time—that damnable time, which has always been the problem of Italian provincial life—passed very pleasantly.

2

Nothing arouses the inquisitive interest of small respectable communities more than an honest effort to keep separate one's public and private lives. What happened to Athos Fadigati after the nurse had shut the door and windows of his surgery behind the last patient? The ambiguous, or at least unusual, use he made of his evenings continuously stimulated people's curiosity about him. Yes, there was something not perfectly clear about Fadigati. But even this, in him, became likeable, even this was attractive.

Everyone knew how he spent his mornings, and no one had the smallest comment to make on the subject.

At nine he was already at the hospital, and visits and operations (because he operated, too: not a day passed without some tonsils to remove or a mastoid to cut) went on continuously till one o'clock. After which, between one and two, it was not unusual to meet him walking along Corso Giovecca with a packet of tunny in oil or of cold meat hanging on his little finger, and the *Corriere della Sera* sticking out of the pocket of his overcoat. Which meant he had lunch at home. And as he had no cook, and the nurse came only in the afternoon, he must have prepared the indispensable plate of *pasta* himself, which in itself was something pretty odd.

At supper too it would have been useless to expect him in the only two or three respectable restaurants in town: the *Vincenzo*, the *Sandrina*, the *Three Cocks*, or even the *Roverara*, in Vicolo del Granchio, whose home cooking attracted so many other middle-aged bachelors. But this was no indication that he ate at home, as he did for lunch. He was hardly ever at home in the evenings. If you went down Via Gorgadello about eight or a quarter past, it was easy to catch him just as he was going out. He would pause a moment on the doorstep, and look up, then left, then right, as if uncertain of the weather and the direction he meant to take; then at last set off, mingling with the flow of people who, at that hour, winter and summer, moved slowly along before the lighted windows of Via Bersaglieri del Po, as along a Venetian draper's.

Where did he go? Wandering about haphazardly

here and there, apparently without any precise end in view.

After a hard day's work he liked to feel himself in the crowd: the gay, noisy, neutral crowd. Tall and fat, with his soft hat, his yellow gloves and, in winter, his long loose cloak lined with opossum and his walking-stick hooked into the right pocket beside the sleeve, between eight and nine in the evening he might be seen anywhere in town. Sometimes you might be surprised to see him standing in front of a shop-window in Via Mazzini or Via Saraceno, peering intently over the shoulders of the man in front of him. Often he stood by the stands of knick-knacks and sweets that spread in dozens along the south side of the cathedral, or in Piazza Travaglio, or in Via Garibaldi, staring silently at the unpretentious goods on show. But the narrow, crowded pavements of Via San Romano were those that Fadigati liked best. By those low doorways, smelling acridly of fried fish, salted foods, wine, and cheap rope, and crowded with girls and soldiers, boys and cloaked peasants, it was strange to see his gay, lively, satisfied look, when you met him, and the vague smile that lit up his face.

"Good evening, doctor," someone would call out after him.

And it was a miracle if he heard, if, already borne

away on the current, he turned to answer the greeting.

It was only later, after ten, that he reappeared in one of the four cinemas in town: the *Excelsior*, the *Salvini*, the *Rex* or the *Diana*. But here, too, he preferred the back rows of the stalls to those upstairs where smart people always met as if they were in a drawing-room. And how embarrassing it was for those same smart people to see him, so well dressed, mixing below with all the very lowest of the rabble! Was it really in good taste—they sighed, looking regretfully away—to go quite so far in showing his bohemian spirit?

And so it was quite understandable that towards 1930, when Fadigati was already over forty, a good many people began to think he ought to get married pretty soon. Patients, their armchairs huddled together, murmured about it in his very flat at Via Gorgadello, while they waited for the unwitting doctor to appear at the door reserved for his periodic appearances to invite them to come through "beyond". Later, at supper, husbands and wives would bring it up again, taking care that the children, with noses in the soup and ears cocked, should not guess what they were talking about. And later, in bed, and now talking unreservedly, the subject regularly took up five or ten minutes of those precious half-

16

hours given over to confidences and ever lengthening yawns, that generally precede the exchange of kisses and "good nights".

It seemed as absurd to the husbands as it did to their wives that a man of his quality should not get down to starting a family right away.

Apart from his slightly "artistic" nature, which on the whole was so serious and so calm, what other professional man in Ferrara on the right side of fifty could boast a better position than his? Everyone liked him, he was rich (as far as money went, he must have been earning whatever he liked!); a member of the two most important clubs in town, and accepted alike by the middle and lower middle classes of professional men and shopkeepers and by the aristocracy, either crested or not, that lived off land and private incomes; even a member of the Fascist party, since, although he had modestly declared he was "non-political by nature", the Federal Secretary himself had been very keen to make him one. What did he lack except a pretty woman to take to San Carlo or the cathedral on Sunday mornings, and in the evening to the cinema, jewelled and befurred as she should be? And why wasn't he looking round for one? Maybe that was it—maybe he was involved with a woman he couldn't acknowledge—some dressmaker, or housekeeper, or servant. Perhaps, as so often happens with doctors, he liked only nurses—and perhaps for this very reason those who worked for him year after year in his surgery were always so pert and pretty! But even supposing this was really the case—on the other hand it was odd that nothing definite had ever slipped out on the subject—why did he still not marry? Did he really want to end up like Dr. Elia Corcos, eighty-year-old head of the hospital and the outstanding doctor in Ferrara, who, people said, after making love to a young nurse for years, had been forced by her family to keep her on for the rest of her life?

The girl really worthy to become Signora Fadigati was already being searched for enthusiastically in town (but every girl who came up seemed unsuitable for one reason or another, no one seemed exactly right for the solitary man who, some evenings, came out in a crowd from the *Excelsior* or the *Salvini* in Piazza delle Erbe, and would suddenly turn up at the end of the Listone, a moment before vanishing into the dark cutting of Via Bersaglieri del Po . . .) when very odd rumours began going about—first bruited no one knew where—about this odd doctor.

"Don't you know? It seems that Dr. Fadigati is . . ."

"Just listen to this. You know Dr. Fadigati, who lives in Via Gorgadello, almost at the corner of Via Bersaglieri del Po? Well, I've heard it said that . . ."

3

A gesture, a grimace was enough.

It was enough to say that Fadigati was "like that", that he was "one of those".

But sometimes, as happens in talking of something improper, and of sexual inversion in particular, someone would grin and use a word in dialect, which is always much harsher than the language of the upper classes. And then add, with a touch of melancholy:

"Well, that's how it is."

"What a man, though."

"Why didn't we think of it before?"

They smiled, all the same. As if they were not too sorry to have noticed Dr. Fadigati's weakness so late in the day (imagine, it had taken them more than ten years to notice it!) but, in a way, reassured.

In fact, they exclaimed, shrugging their shoulders, one had to admit that even in the most shameful irregularity the man had style.

What most persuaded them to be indulgent towards Fadigati, and, after the first moment of alarmed bewilderment, almost to admire him, was just this question of his style. By style they meant chiefly one thing: his discretion, the way he had always been so obviously careful—and continued being so—to hide his tastes, not to give scandal. Yes, they said: now that his secret was no longer a secret, now that everything about him was clear, they knew at last how to treat him. By day, in the sunlight, to take off their hats to him at once; at night, even if it meant squeezing up against the crowd in Via San Romano, to look as if he was a stranger. Like Fredric March in *Dr. Jekyll and Mr. Hyde*, Dr. Fadigati had two lives. But who hasn't?

Knowing meant understanding, not being curious any longer, letting the matter drop.

Before, when they went to the cinema, the thing that most bothered them—they recalled—was discovering if *he* was in the back as usual. They knew his habits, they had noticed he never sat down. Peering into the darkness over the gallery balustrade, they searched for him below along the dirty side walls near the doors of the safety exits and the lavatories. They could not understand his behaviour, and for this very reason, perhaps, could not rest till they had caught the characteristic gleam of his gold-rimmed spectacles now and then across the smoke and the darkness: a small uncertain gleam, proof of a really infinite remoteness. . . . But now! What was the point, now, of having his presence confirmed the moment they arrived? And besides, why be embarrassed, as they once had been, every time the lights went up in the cinema? If there was one professional man in Ferrara whose right to sit in the low-class stalls and sink openly into the dreadful underworld of seats at one lira twenty was acknowledged, that man was Fadigati.

The same thing happened at the Merchants' Club and the Concordi on the two or three evenings of the year that he went there (as I have already said, he had been a member of both clubs since 1927).

In the past, as he went through the billiard room, and continued without pausing by the tables of poker or ecarté, every face at once took on an expression halfway between consternation and surprise; but now it was different: and very few looked up from the green cloths to follow his progress to the library door. He could shut himself up happily in the library, where there was never a soul, where the leather armchairs reflected the tremulous glimmers from the fireplace, and till midnight or later bury himself in a scientific book which he brought from home: who now found anything to object to in strange behaviour of the sort?

There was more to it than that. Every now and then he went on a trip, or, in his own words, he allowed himself "an escape": to Venice for the Biennale, to Florence for the Maggio. Well, now that people knew, they could meet him on the train in the middle of the night, as a small group from Ferrara did in 1934 after a trip to Florence for a football match, without anyone saying maliciously "Look who's here!" the way people from Ferrara always do the moment they meet anyone outside the narrow strip of land between the silver parallels of the Po and the Reno. Those good sportsmen invited him gushingly to share their compartment, and, though they were anything but musical (Wagner: the very name was enough to plunge them into gloom!), they sat there as quiet as mice, listening to Fadigati's fervent account of the *Tristan* that Bruno Walter had conducted at the Comunale in Florence that same afternoon. Fadigati spoke of the music of *Tristan*, of the marvellous interpretation the "German master" had given it, but above all of the second act, which, he said, "is nothing but a long lament of love". He spoke of the bench, an obvious symbol of the marriage bed, where the lovers sit and sing for three-quarters of an hour on end. As he went on about the bench, about the roses surrounding it, about Tristan and Isolda's night of love—their sub-

23

lime, their *ewige Nacht*—Fadigati half-closed his eyes behind his glasses, and smiled enraptured. And the others let him carry on, without breathing. All they did was exchange a few looks.

But it was Fadigati himself, and his formally un-exceptional behaviour, that aroused such a generous spirit of tolerance.

And after all, what could be said that was in any way concrete about him? Unlike the behaviour of, say, Laura Grillenzoni, a woman in the highest circles and over seventy, whose impetuous seduction of chemists' or butchers' boys who called at her house in the morning was heard of all over town (every now and then something new came out about her and people laughed, of course, but deplored it too), Fadigati's behaviour was guaranteed to remain, quite definitely, within the limits of decency.

His many friends and admirers were absolutely certain of this. Of course they had to admit that in the cinema he always went at once near some groups of soldiers: which meant rumours went about that he had a "weakness for the military". But on the other hand, they went on to say energetically, the poor fellow had never been seen nearer the sol-diers than that, had never been seen walking along the street with one; still less had any young Pinerolo cavalryman, with tall busby pulled down over his eyes and heavy clanking sabre under his arm, been seen to leave his house at suspicious hours. All that remained was his face: fat but grey, its features wrenched by a secret and continuous anguish. Only his face reminded one he was *searching*. But as for his ever finding (how and where), who was in a position to tell?

From time to time, all the same, we did hear talk of this too. At intervals of several years, as slowly and reluctantly as rare bubbles of air rise from the muddy depths to break silently on the surface of a bog, names came out occasionally—names attached to real people and definite circumstances.

Around 1935, I remember well that Fadigati's name was usually linked with that of a policeman with inflexible blue eyes, called Manservigi, who, when he was not standing officiously on point duty at the crossing between Corso Roma and Corso Giovecca, we boys were sometimes surprised to find on the Montagnone, almost unrecognizable out of uniform, and with a toothpick in his mouth watching our interminable football matches, that often went on into the evening. Later, about '36, we heard of someone else: a doorman at the town hall, called Trapolini, a gentle, soft-spoken man, married and with a tribe of children, and already known in town for his zeal as a Catholic and his passion for the opera. Later still, during the first months of the war in Spain, the name of an ex-footballer from the U.S. Estense team was added to the short list of Fadigati's friends. Dark-skinned, gone to seed, grey at the temples, it was in fact Baùsi, Olao Baùsi, who in the ten years between 1920 and 1930 had been (and who could forget it?) a kind of idol to young sportsmen in Ferrara, and in a few years was reduced to living by the direst expedients.

Well, so there were no soldiers. Nothing public, not even the first phases, nothing scandalous, ever. Just carefully hidden relationships with middle-aged men, in modest, subordinate positions. With men who were discreet, in fact, or at least somehow made to be so.

Around three or four in the morning, a little light always filtered through the shutters of Fadigati's flat. In the silence of the alley, which was interrupted only by the strange sighs of owls nesting high along the dizzy and barely visible cornices of the cathedral, flew little puffs of heavenly music, Bach, Mozart, Beethoven, Wagner. Wagner above all, perhaps because his music best conjured a particular atmosphere. The idea that the policeman Manservigi, or the doorman Trapolini, or the ex-footballer Baùsi, might at that very moment be the doctor's guest, could not occur to the last night prowler who passed down Via Gorgadello at that hour, except light-heartedly.

4

In 1936, exactly twenty years ago, the local train leaving Ferrara every morning a few minutes before seven o'clock covered the forty-five kilometres of railway line between Ferrara and Bologna in not less than an hour and twenty minutes.

When everything went smoothly, the train reached Bologna at a quarter-past eight. But more often than not, even if it shot along the line after Corticella, it turned into the long curve before Bologna station ten or fifteen minutes late. (When it was signalled to stop at the entrance the minutes might even climb to thirty.) We were then no longer in the days of old Ciano, of course, when trains sometimes found the Minister of Communications waiting for them in person when they arrived, marching impatiently up and down the platform and every minute checking the time on a large watch which he pulled out of his waistcoat pocket.

And the fact was, the 6.50 train did exactly what it pleased. It seemed to know nothing about the government and its boast that it had given even the state railways a respect for time-tables; and, as far as the government was concerned, this was a case when it seemed ready to shut, not just one eye, but both. The local train from Ferrara first thing in the morning could reach Bologna station half an hour late or more: who cared, who worried? Half-covered in grass, roofless platform 16, where it belonged, was the last one in the station, and met the countryside outside Porta Galliera. It really looked as if it had been forgotten.

Usually the train consisted of only six carriages: five third-class and one second-class.

I remember the December mornings in Ferrara, the dark mornings of our student years when we had to be called by alarm-clock. From the tram which dashed along at break-neck speed towards the toll gate in Viale Cavour we could hear the train whistling repeatedly, far and invisible. "Look out, I'm off!" it seemed to be threatening us. Or even: "No good hurrying, chaps, I've left already." But the only people who urged the conductor to hurry were the first-year students, boys and girls. The rest of us, including Eraldo Deliliers, who had started at Bologna in political science that same year, but behaved with the casualness and indifference of an old hand, knew the 6.50 would never leave Ferrara before picking us all up. The tram finally stopped before the station, and we jumped down; and after a few minutes got on to the train that was puffing white tufts of steam on every side, but standing quite still on the line, as we had foreseen it would be. Deliliers always came last, walking very slowly and yawning. It often happened, in fact, that as he had gone to sleep we had to pull him off the tram by main force.

The third-class carriages were to all intents and purposes ours. Apart from the odd commercial traveller or meagre troops of actors that had spent the night in the station waiting-room (we sometimes tried to get friendly with the women dancers on the journey), no one left Ferrara at that hour.

But this certainly doesn't mean that the 6.50 ran half-empty most of the journey!

During its lazy journey from the heavy darkness of Ferrara to the morning light of Bologna—an intense, glittering light, some days, with the hill of San Luca white with snow, and the greenish cupolas of the churches glittering almost in outline in the red sea of towers and roofs—the train gradually picked up new passengers at the tiny unimportant stations strung along the line.

There were high-school students, boys and girls;

primary school teachers of both sexes; small land-owners, tenant farmers, cattle dealers you could recognize from their big cloaks, and felt hats pulled down over their eyes, and the toothpick or cigarette stub stuck between their lips; country folk, who spoke the oafish dialect of Bologna, and from whose company we defended ourselves by barricading ourselves into two or three adjoining compartments. They began their assault at Poggio Renatico, a kilometre beyond the left bank of the Reno; started it up again at Galliera, just after the iron bridge, then at San Giorgio di Piano, at San Pietro in Casale, at Castelmaggiore, at Corticella. When the train reached Bologna, from the doors flung open with almost explosive violence there tumbled out on to platform 16 a small noisy crowd of several hundred.

There remained the single, solitary second-class carriage; from which, until a certain date, that is until the winter of 1936–37, not a soul ever emerged.

The staff in charge of the train, four of them who never changed, did the journey between Ferrara and Bologna five or six times a day, and every morning played cards in it. And we were so used to the fact that the second-class carriage was in practice reserved for the head of the train, the ticket collector, the brakeman, and the railway policeman (friendly and nice as could be, all four of them, especially if they sniffed out students of the G.U.F., but very definite in forbidding us to travel on the wrong tickets); it seemed to us so natural, I mean to say, to see it used as a club for the railway staff that at first when Dr. Fadigati began coming to Bologna twice a week and always took a second-class ticket, at first we didn't realize, and never even noticed him.

But not for long.

If I close my eyes I can see the great paved sweep of the Viale Cavour completely deserted from the Castle to the toll gate, the street lamps, set at about fifty yards' distance from one another, all still alight. Aldrovandi, the tram-driver, invisible from the inside of the tram except for his hunched and irritated back, urged his decrepit vehicle as fast as it would go. But just a moment before the train reached the barrier a taxi swooped down on us and swept past with the characteristic muffled swoosh of its Lancia motor; a green Astura, always the same one. Every Tuesday and Friday morning at about the same point on the Viale Cavour it passed us. And it went so fast that when our tram rolled alarmingly along in its final sprint, and burst into the station yard, it had not only dropped its passenger (a corpulent gentleman wearing a soft hat with a white edge to its brim, gold-rimmed spectacles, and a fur-collared overcoat) but had already turned and was leaving in

31

the opposite direction towards the middle of town.

Which one of us was it who first called attention to the passenger: to the passenger, that is, rather than to the taxi? The fact is that in the tram, his curly blond head lying back on the wooden back of the seat, Deliliers usually slept. And yet I have a feeling that it was actually he, one morning about the middle of February in 1937, as several hands, always rather more than necessary, were leaning out across the tram door to help him climb down, and he was making us lift him almost bodily; yes, I could swear it was in fact Deliliers who declared that the second-class had found a regular customer in the man who came in the Astura, a rich and regular customer, who was none other than Dr. Fadigati.

"Fadigati? Who is he?" one of the girls asked bewilderedly; Bianca Scarbi, actually, the elder of the two Scarbi girls (the other, Attilia, three years younger and still at high school, I didn't yet know at the beginning of '37).

Roars of laughter greeted her question. Deliliers had sat down and was lighting up a cigarette. He had a mania for lighting his cigarettes at the end where the trade mark was written, and was always very careful not to do otherwise.

In those days Bianca Scarbi, who was very reluctantly reading literature in her third year at the

university, was almost engaged to Nino Bottecchiari, nephew of the ex-socialist deputy. Although
they went around together, as we say in Ferrara, they
didn't get on too well. Exuberant by nature, and as
if she foretold the sad future that awaited the young
people of our generation, and her own in particular
(she married an Air Force officer who crashed over
Malta in 1942, and with two young sons ended up,
poor thing, in Rome with a job at the Ministry of
Aeronautics), she seemed unable to stand any sort of
constraint, and amused herself flirting with anyone
she liked, in fact going from one flirtation to another.

"Well then, will you tell me who he is?" Bianca
insisted softly, leaning towards Deliliers who was
sitting in front of her.

Pushed up against Deliliers, in the corner seat by
the door, poor Nino suffered in silence.

"Oh he's an old pansy," Deliliers eventually said,
looking up and staring her straight in the eyes.

5

For a time he kept segregated for the entire
journey in the second-class carriage.

Taking advantage of the stops the train made
at San Giorgio di Piano or at San Pietro in Casale,
we took it in turns to jump down and buy something to eat at the station bars: rolls newly filled
with raw salame, chocolate with almonds, that
tasted of soap, half-mouldy Osvego biscuits. And if
we looked back at the stationary train, we saw Dr.
Fadigati at once behind the thick windows of his
carriage, watching people crossing the lines and
hurrying back to the third-class compartment.
From the expression of heartfelt envy on his face,
from the regretful looks with which he followed the
movements of the small rural crowd we found such
a bore, he seemed little less than a recluse: some important prisoner being transferred to Ponza or
Tremiti to stay there heaven knows how long. Two

or three carriages farther along, behind an equally thick window, we could make out the engine-driver and his friends, who carried on with their card games imperturbably, chattering hard among themselves, laughing and waving their hands.

In any case very soon, as we might have foreseen, we began to see him wandering through the third-class carriages. The communicating door was always locked, and to get it open (he told us himself later) he had to ask the ticket collector every time.

"Excuse me, gentlemen," he asked, putting his head into the gambling den, "might I please go into the third-class?"

But it annoyed them, he realized only too well. The ticket collector would march ahead of him down the corridor like a prison warder, key in hand, muttering and breathing rudely. After a while Fadigati decided to do it on his own. He waited for the first stop, the one at Poggio Renatico, where the train stopped for three to five minutes. There was plenty of time to get out and climb up again into the next compartment.

In spite of this, it was not in the train that we first made contact with him; no, I'm quite certain it wasn't. I have a feeling it happened in Bologna, in the street, even though, as you will see, I cannot say quite definitely *which* street. (Perhaps I was away from the university for a few days, and the others told me about it afterwards. Or is it simply at this distance I cannot distinguish things or remember them very precisely?)

It may have taken place as we were leaving the station, while we waited for the tram. There were about ten of us altogether taking up most of the platform tram stop beside the parking place for carriages and taxis. The sun was glittering on the mounds of dirty snow scattered at regular intervals in the enormous square, and the sky above was an intense blue, glittering with light.

And Fadigati, who was waiting for the tram too on the same platform (he had arrived last, a moment ago) suddenly could find nothing better to start up a conversation than some platitude like: "What a heavenly day, almost like spring," or else something about the tram, which was "so much trouble to catch it would really be better value to walk". They were rather commonplace generalizations, spoken softly and addressed to no one in particular; to all of us in a group and yet to nobody special, as if he didn't really know us, or rather as if he didn't dare admit that he knew us, even by sight. And in the end someone, embarrassed by his uncertainty and by the nervous smile that went with his vague remarks on the weather or the tram, answered him with a minimum of politeness, and called him "doctor". And then the truth came out: that he knew us all perfectly well, our surnames and our Christian names, in spite of the fact that, in the last few years, we had all grown up. He knew exactly who our fathers were; and how could he fail to, how could he have forgotten, after all, since as children, "at the age when all well-bred children have sore throats and bad ears" (he laughed), he had seen us come into his surgery, every one of us?

Often instead of taking the tram and going direct to the university in Via Zamboni, we preferred to walk along the porticoes of Via Indipendenza, into the middle of town. Deliliers very seldom came with us. As soon as he left the station he cut away on his own, and usually no one saw him, at the university or in a restaurant, or anywhere else, until the following morning. But the rest of us were always there, scattered about the pavements. There was Nino Bottecchiari, who was studying law, but, because of Bianca Scarbi, kept haunting the corridors and lecture rooms of the faculty of literature, patiently taking in the most indigestible lectures, from Latin grammar to librarianship. There was Bianca in a blue beret and hip-length rabbit-skin coat, arm in arm with one boy or another: hardly ever with Nino, and then only quarrelling with him.

There was Sergio Pavani, Otello Forti, Giovannino Piazza, Enrico Sangiuliano, Vittorio Molon: some of them agricultural students, some medical students, some economists, some studying commerce. And finally there was myself who, apart from Bianca Scarbi, was the only one of us all reading literature.

Well then, it was not at all surprising that one of those mornings, as we walked along the interminable porticoes of the Indipendenza, that were as high and dark as a church nave, stopping every now and then in front of a sports' shop window, or by a newspaper kiosk, or mixing with a group who, attracted and hypnotized by the oxygen flame, made a silent hedge round a group of workmen repairing a fault in the tram-lines; as I was saying, it was not at all surprising that one of these mornings, late in winter, when every excuse seems good enough to put off the moment when you must shut yourself up in a lecture room, Dr. Fadigati, who for some time had been following us, came imperceptibly up to one of us, up to Nino or Bianca, say, who a little apart, but as usual not caring who heard them, were arguing and quarrelling together.

Fadigati had been following us from the station, buzzing round us continuously, you might say. We had realized perfectly well, of course, had grinned and nudged each other and remarked on it.

Suddenly he went up to Nino and Bianca and cleared his throat. In his neutral voice, in the vaguely impersonal tone he always used when he met people he didn't know, whose welcome he wasn't sure of, we heard him say something.

"Come now, my dears!" he admonished them: and even then it seemed as if he was talking to the air, not to anyone in particular.

Then, looking round at Bianca in a timid and hesitant way, yet rather as if he was her unwilling accomplice, and supporting her, he said:

"And you be nice, my dear; be a little more submissive. It's a woman's business, don't you know."

The poor man was only joking, that was all he meant. Bianca burst out laughing. Nino laughed too. Then, all together, chattering about this and that, we reached Piazza del Nettuno. What's more, before we separated we had to accept a cup of coffee from him.

And so we became friends. In any case the fact is that from the end of April 1937, in the two or three third-class carriages where we barricaded ourselves (the landscape flashing fresh and luminous beyond the square of window), on Tuesday and Friday mornings there was always a seat for Dr. Fadigati.

6

He had made up his mind to take an advanced degree, he said, and for this reason went to Bologna twice a week. But now he had found company on the journey, this bi-weekly trek no longer bothered him much.

He sat quietly in his seat, just listening to our usual discussions, that wandered from sport to politics, from literature to philosophy, and sometimes even touched on love; every now and then he put in a word or two, and looked at us from his seat with a fatherly and indulgent eye. In a way he was a family friend of many of us; our parents had been to his surgery in Via Gorgadello for nearly twenty years. No doubt he was thinking of them as he looked at us.

Did he know *we knew*? Perhaps not, perhaps he still fooled himself about this. Yet in his manner, in the polite and worried reserve which he forced himself to retain, it was all too easy to see his firm decision to behave as if nothing had ever been heard about him in town. To us, above all to us, he must continue to be the one-time Dr. Fadigati whose broad face we had seen as children half-hidden by the round mirror on his forehead as he leant over our faces. If there was anyone on earth with whom he must try to keep his end up, it was us.

Seen close to, his face had not greatly changed. Those ten or twelve years which now separated us from the age of tonsillitis and ear trouble and adenoids had left only very slight traces on his face. They had made him grey at the temples, that was all. But as for the rest, his cheeks were a little fatter, they drooped a bit more, perhaps, but they were the same rosy colour as before, still smooth and fat, with open pores, still giving the same impression of well-kept leather. No, if it came to that we had changed a great deal more than he had, we who secretly and absurdly (when he occasionally pulled a newspaper from his overcoat pocket, and, quiet and good-natured in his corner, began to read it), were trying to find in that familiar face of his the proofs and marks, I might say the visible stains, of his vice, of his sin.

With time he became more confident, all the same, and began to talk a little more. After a short spring, the summer came almost suddenly. Even early in the morning it was hot. Outside, the green of the countryside had grown darker and richer: in the fields edged by rows of mulberry trees, the hemp was already tall, the corn already yellow.

"I feel like a student again," Fadigati often said, looking out. "I feel I'm back at the time when I used to travel up and down between Venice and Padua. . . ."

It had been before the 1915-18 war, he said, between 1910 and 1915.

He was doing medicine at Padua, and for two years had travelled between the two cities every day, more or less the same distance as we went between Ferrara and Bologna. At the beginning of the third year, though, his parents, who were always anxious about his heart, wanted him to stay at Padua, in a rented room. And so, for the three next years (he qualified in 1915), he led a relatively sedentary life, compared with the previous years. But every Saturday morning he took the train to spend the weekend with his family. Certainly Venice was hardly gay in those days, on Sundays and especially in winter. But Padua, with its gloomy dark porticoes, with the smell of stew that hung about on holidays, floating out of restaurants . . . besides he had to be punctual at lectures on Mondays.

"What an old swot you must have been, doctor!"
Bianca once exclaimed; it had become so much of a
habit with her that she even flirted with Fadigati.

He didn't answer her directly, just smiled at her
kindly.

"Nowadays you have your football matches, your
cinemas, all sorts of healthy occupations," he said
later. "D'you know what the main refuge of young
people in my day was on Sundays? The dance hall!"

He twisted his mouth as he said this, as if he had
been speaking of somewhere simply abominable;
and added at once that at Venice at least he had his
home, his father and mother, above all his mother:
the holiest affections, in fact.

How he adored her, he sighed, his poor mother!

Intelligent, cultivated, beautiful, pious: she had
all the virtues. One morning he even took from his
wallet, and as he did so his eyes filled with tears, a
photograph which passed rapidly from hand to
hand. It was a small faded oval picture of a middle-
aged woman in nineteenth-century clothes, with a
gentle expression, yes, but on the whole rather
ordinary.

Vittorio Molon was the only one of us whose
family was not from Ferrara. The Molons were land-
owners from Fratta Polesine who had come here
from the Po only five or six years before. And you

43

could hear it, because Vittorio still had the Venetian lilt in his voice, especially when he was not using dialect. One day Fadigati asked him if by any chance his family came from Padua.

"I'm asking," he explained, "because when I was living in Padua I lodged with a widow called Molon, Elsa Molon. The little house this Signora Molon lived in was in Via San Francesco, near the university, and it gave on to a big garden at the back. What a strange life I led! I had no relatives or friends at Padua, not even among my fellow students."

After this, apparently wandering off the point (but it was the only time he shed a gleam of light on his considerable literary culture: it was as if there was some definite embargo placed on that side of him too), he began talking of a story by some nineteenth-century English or American writer which was set in Padua about the sixteenth century, he remembered well.

"The main character in this story", he said, "is a solitary student like myself thirty years ago. Like me he lived in a rented room which looked out on to a big garden full of poisonous trees. . ."

"Poisonous!" interrupted Bianca, her blue eyes opening wide.

"Poisonous," he said. "The garden on to which my window opened certainly wasn't poisonous though, you can be sure of that. It was a very ordinary garden, beautifully kept by a family of peasants called Scagnellato, that lived in a little house beside the apse of the church of San Francesco. I often went down to walk there with a book in my hand, especially in the late afternoons in July when we had exams. The family often invited me to supper, they were the only family in Padua I became friendly with. They had two sons, two handsome boys, so alive and so charming, so. . . . They worked among the plants and the crops till the light was gone. At that hour they were generally watering the garden. Oh, the good smell of manure!"

The air of the carriage was grey with the smoke of our cigarettes, but he was breathing it in deeply, his eyes half shut behind his spectacles, the nostrils of his fat nose opened wide.

There was a rather long and oppressive silence. Deliliers opened his eyes and yawned noisily.

"The good smell of manure?" Bianca said with a nervous little laugh. "What an idea!"

Sticking his head forward, Deliliers gave Fadigati a scornful look. "Don't worry about the manure, doctor," he sneered. "Tell us instead about those two boys in the garden you liked so much. What did you do with them?"

Fadigati gave a jerk. As if he had been suddenly

struck a tremendous blow, his wide face changed under our very eyes with a grimace of pain.

"What . . . what d'you mean?" he stammered.

Deliliers got up disgustedly, and pushed his way roughly between our legs into the corridor.

"Beast, as usual," burst out Bianca, touching her knee.

She flung Deliliers, who stood exiled in the corridor beyond the glass door, a look of disapproval. Then, turning to Fadigati, she suggested kindly:

"Why don't you finish telling us about the story?"

He wouldn't, though, however much Bianca pressed him; protesting that he couldn't remember the plot exactly. And besides, he concluded with a trace of melancholy gallantry that sounded particularly forced, why would she want to hear a story which he could assure her ended extremely badly?

Letting go for just one moment had cost him dear. Now, of course, he feared ridicule more than ever.

7

He was happy with so very little, or so it seemed. He asked no more than to stay there, in our third-class compartment, with the air of an old man warming himself in silence at a fire.

At Bologna, for instance, as soon as we came out of the underground passage into the square in front of the station, he took a taxi and left. After the first time or two at the beginning, when he came with us as far as the university, we never met him without being able to get rid of him. He knew perfectly well, because we had told him, the cheap restaurants where he could have found us around one o'clock: the *North Star*, in Strada Maggiore, or the *Gigino*, at the foot of the two Towers, or the *Farmyard Hen*, in San Vitale. But as far as I remember he never did. When we went into a café in Via Zamboni one afternoon to play at billiards, we found him sitting on his own at a table, with a cup of coffee and a glass of water before him, deep in a newspaper. He realized at once that it was us, of course. But he pretended not to; what's more, after a few minutes he called the waiter with a gesture, paid and slipped out furtively.

The fact was, he was neither obtrusive or annoying.

Yet gradually, in spite of the fact that, being so fat, he had to huddle up on the wooden bench of the compartment so as to take up only an eighth of it or even less, gradually, without meaning to, most of us began treating him rudely.

It was he who made the first mistake, actually. One morning while the train was stopping at San Pietro in Casale, he suddenly began to get off, heaven knows why, to buy the usual rolls and biscuits at the station bar. "It's my turn," he said, and we couldn't stop him.

From the train we saw him clumsily crossing the lines. We could have betted he had forgotten how many rolls he should buy and how many packets of biscuits. And, in fact, it turned out exactly as we had foreseen. So there were we, hanging out of the window like drunken conscripts, uncontrollably grinning and shouting contradictory orders from a distance; while he grew more and more confused and breathless as the minutes passed, and only just caught the train by the skin of his teeth.

Then there was Deliliers, who hardly ever spoke to him, and every time he did brought out the most obvious allusions and brutal innuendoes to hurt him. But even Nino Bottecchiari, whose tonsils he had taken out as a child, and who was the only one of us he called by the familiar *tu*, began treating him coldly. And what about him? It was strange to see him and also painful: the ruder Nino and Deliliers were to him, the more he vainly tried to make them like him. For one kind word, one friendly glance, one amused smile from one of them he would have done anything. With Nino, who was unanimously considered the intellectual of the group, and the previous year had taken part in a congress of Culture and Art at Venice (he came fifth in fascist doctrine and second in film criticism), he tried to start discussions that would give him a chance of shining: on the cinema, or even on politics—though, as he had said definitely several times, he didn't know much about politics.

But he was unlucky. He never quite brought it off.

He would start talking about the cinema (he really knew something about it: for years he had spent every evening in the cinema!) and Nino would land on him hysterically at once, as if he refused to admit even his right to talk about it, as if to hear him say something like . . . oh, I don't know, that the old comedies of Ridolini were "stupendous", say, was enough to make him change his mind absolutely on the subject.

Rebuffed, Fadigati would then try politics. The war in Spain was now nearly over, with victory for Franco and fascism. One morning, looking at the first page of the newspaper, and certain he was not saying anything Nino or anyone else there could possibly dislike, but convinced he would find us all agreeing with him, he expressed the view—certainly not an unusual one at the time—that the imminent victory of "our legions" was something pretty fine. And then, without warning, the most unforeseeable thing imaginable happened. As if he had had an electric shock, raising his voice so much that at one point Bianca tried to cover his mouth with her hand, Nino began saying that maybe it was a disaster and maybe the beginning of the end: and that as far as he was concerned he, at his age, was ashamed to have been so "irresponsible".

"I'm sorry, dear boy, please do listen . . ." Fadigati tried to say, pale as a corpse. The attack bewildered him, he couldn't understand it, and looked round as if to ask for an explanation. But we too were much too upset to take any notice, I above all, because the previous year, during one of our usual discussions, I had been accused by Nino himself (an ardent supporter of the ethical state!) of being imbued with "Crocian scepticism" . . . . And then, after all, were the doctor's round eyes really terrified, or were they not shining brilliantly behind his glasses, full of bitter satisfaction, of childish, inexplicable blind gaiety?

Another time we were all discussing sport, Deliliers among us.

If Nino was thought to be our number one in matters of culture, Deliliers was undoubtedly outstanding in sport. He belonged to Ferrara only through his mother (his father had come from Imperia, I think, or from Ventimiglia, and was in the war in 1918 at the head of a company of Arditi), and he, like Vittorio, had been in Ferrara only for his high-school years—four years in the science high school, that is. But, in any case, these four years were enough to make Eraldo, who in 1935 had won the schoolboys' regional championship, middleweight category, and apart from this was superbly handsome, about six feet tall and with the face and body of a Greek statue, into a real local hero. He was still under twenty, yet was already credited with three or four much-talked-about conquests. One of the girls at school, who had committed suicide the same year as he won the championship title, had done it for love of him, it was said. He suddenly jilted her, people said; and she ran and flung herself in the river, poor thing. The fact was that even among us, in our student circle, Eraldo Deliliers was not just loved but downright idolized. We copied the way he dressed, the clothes his mother tirelessly brushed and cleaned and ironed. And to stand beside him on Sunday morning leaning against a column of the Caffè portico and watching the women's legs go by, was generally considered a privilege.

Well, once in the train, towards the end of May, we were discussing sport with Deliliers. From athletics we went on to boxing. Deliliers never talked much to anybody. But that day he opened out a good deal. He said he wasn't too keen on this sort of work as a student, and that just living was far too expensive; and so if a certain little "wangle" he was thinking about came off, he would take up boxing altogether.

"Professionally?" Fadigati ventured to ask him.

Deliliers looked at him as if he was a scarecrow.

"Of course," he said. "Are you afraid I might ruin my face, doctor?"

"I don't mind about your face," said Fadigati, "and in any case I can see your eyebrows are already badly scarred. But I do think it's my duty to warn you that boxing, especially when it's practised professionally, is bad for the whole organism in the long run. If I were in the government I'd forbid it, even amateur boxing. I think it's legalized murder, not sport. Sheer organized brutality."

"Now look here," interrupted Deliliers, "have you ever seen it?"

Fadigati was forced to admit he hadn't. He said that although he was a doctor, he had a horror of violence and blood.

"Well then, if you've never seen any boxing," Deliliers cut him short, raising his voice, "why are you talking? Who asked your opinion, anyway?"

And again, as Deliliers almost shouted these last words, and then, turning his back on him, explained to us much more calmly that boxing, "contrary to what certain idiots might think", depended on the legs, and on timing; it was like fencing, in fact, more than anything like fencing, I saw shining in Fadigati's eyes that absurd but unmistakable light of inner joy.

Nino was the only one of us who did not venerate Deliliers. They were not friends, but they respected each other. When Nino was there Deliliers noticeably tempered his normal gangster-like pose; and with Deliliers Nino became far less donnish.

One morning Nino and Bianca were not there (I think it was in June, during the exams). There were only six of us in the compartment, all of us men.

I complained of a slight sore throat. Remembering that when I was growing fast as a child I had had to be treated for various attacks of tonsillitis, Fadigati at once anxiously offered to have a look.

"Let's see," he said.

He put his glasses up on to his forehead, took my head between his hands, and began gazing down my throat.

"Say aaah," he said.

I did so; and he was still examining my throat, meanwhile recommending me kindly and paternally to look after myself and not to sweat, because my tonsils, though now fairly small, were obviously still my Achilles heel, when Deliliers suddenly came out with:

"Excuse me, doctor; as soon as you've finished, would you mind having a look at me too?"

Fadigati turned, astonished. Astonished at the request, and at the unusually gentle tone in which Deliliers had made it.

"What do you feel?" he asked. "Does it hurt to swallow?"

Deliliers was staring at him with his blue eyes. He smiled, just showing his front teeth.

"I haven't got a sore throat at all," he said.

"Then where does it hurt?" said Fadigati.

"Here," said Deliliers, touching his trousers at the level of the groin.

Then calmly and carelessly, not without a hint of pride, he explained that for about a month he had been suffering from the result of "a present from the virgins of Via Bomporto", something "pretty bloody, if we liked to know"; and because of it he had even had to stop his training at the gym. Dr. Manfredini, he went on, was treating him with blue methylene and daily douches of permanganate. But the treatment was going on and on, and he had to get well as quickly as possible.

"My girls are beginning to complain, you see. And so I wondered, would you be so kind", he said again, "as to have a little peep?"

Fadigati had sat down again.

"But, dear boy," he stammered, "you know perfectly well I don't know anything about that kind of illness. And then, Dr. Manfredini. . . ."

"Come along! Of course you know all about it!" grinned Deliliers.

"Apart from the fact that here in the train . . ." Fadigati went on, gazing at the corridor with alarm, "here in the train . . . how could we? . . ."

"Oh, as far as that's concerned," Deliliers

55

answered, his scornful mouth askew, "there's always the lavatory, if you agree."

There was a moment's silence. Suddenly Fadigati burst out laughing.

"But you're joking!" he cried. "Do you have to keep on joking? You must think me pretty dumb!"

Then, leaning sideways to tap Deliliers's knee with his hand, he said:

"You know, you really must be careful. If not you'll come to a bad end!"

And Deliliers said promptly, but seriously:

"Mind *you* don't, more likely."

A few days later, before we took the train for Ferrara, towards six o'clock in the evening we happened to turn up at Majani's in Via Indipendenza. It was very hot, and Nino suggested we have an ice. Even then, before it was remodernized in 1940, Majani's cake-shop was one of the best in Bologna. It consisted of an enormous half-darkened room, with a single gigantic lamp of Murano glass, hanging from its high, shadowy ceiling, about two or three yards in diameter and shaped like a rose, and lit by a large number of little dusty bulbs, which gave out a very small amount of light below.

The moment we were inside we looked across to the end of the room where we heard laughter.

About twenty youths, most of them in navy blue

sports clothes, were down there, some lolling in chairs, some standing, each one holding an ice-cream cup or a cone. They were talking loudly in all sorts of accents: from Bologna, from Rome, from Venice, from Tuscany. You could tell at once that they were university students of the sort that do very much better at swimming and athletics than at lectures and exams.

Apart from Deliliers, who greeted us at once with a friendly wave across the room, we recognized no one in the group just at first. But after a few minutes, when we were used to the half-light of the room, we made out among them a stout gentleman, sitting beside Deliliers with his back to the entrance. There he sat with his hat on, his hands folded on the knob of his walking-stick, not eating anything; just waiting. Like a soft-hearted father, who has agreed to buy ice-creams for a bunch of his noisy children and nephews, and rather shamefacedly waits in silence for his darling kids to finish licking and sucking just as long as they like, so that later he can take them home. . .

The gentleman, of course, was Dr. Fadigati.

8

That summer, like the one before it, we went on holiday to Riccione, on the nearby Adriatic coast. Every year we did the same. My father had tried vainly to drag us up into the Dolomites, to places he had been to in the war, but in the end he had resigned himself to returning to Riccione, and renting the same small house beside the Grand Hotel. I remember it all very well: myself, my mother, and Fanny, my little sister, going to Riccione on August 10th, with the maid. (Ernesto, my brother, had been in England since the middle of July, living *au pair* with a family in Bath to practise the language.) As for my father, he stayed in town, and was to join us later, as soon as he could get away from his rural labours at Masi Torello.

The very day I arrived I heard at once about Fadigati and Deliliers. On the beach, which even then was crammed with families on holiday from

Ferrara, people were talking of nothing but the pair of them and their scandalous "friendship".

Since the beginning of August they had been seen going from one hotel to another in various seaside towns scattered between Porto Corsini and the Punta di Pesaro. The first time they appeared was at Milano Marittima; from there they went on to the canal port of Cervia, and took a fine room at the Mare e Pineta Hotel. After a week they went on to Cesenatico, at the Britannia Hotel. And then gradually, everywhere they went arousing an enormous amount of noise and gossip, they went to Viserba, to Riccione itself, to Rimini and to Cattolica. They were making the journey by car: a red Alfa Romeo 1750 two-seater, very sporty looking.

Around August 20th they turned up unexpectedly at Riccione, staying at the Grand Hotel as they had done ten days before.

The car was brand new and its motor gave out a kind of snarl. Apart from travelling in it, the two friends went driving in it every afternoon, just at sunset when most bathers left the beach to stroll along the front. Deliliers always drove, fair and sunburnt and dazzlingly handsome in his tight shirts and cream woollen trousers (on the hands that lay negligently on the driving wheel, he wore unimaginably expensive-looking leather gloves), and obviously the car was entirely at the disposal of his every whim. Dr. Athos Fadigati, the well-known professional man from Ferrara, who for the occasion wore a flat tartan beret and a pair of mechanic's goggles, as if he was a substitute driver (goggles he never removed, even if the car had to crawl at walking pace along the road in front of the café Zanarini), merely rode up and down, stuck in the seat beside his companion.

They still slept in the same room, and ate at the same table. In the evenings, too, they sat at the same little table when the Grand Hotel orchestra, having carried its instruments from the dining-room down to the outside terrace, exposed to the sea breezes, changed abruptly from light music to jazz. The terrace soon filled up (I often went myself with new friends I had made at the seaside), and Deliliers never missed a tango or a waltz, a quickstep or a slow foxtrot. Fadigati never danced, of course. Every now and then he pressed to his lips the little stick he had taken out of his drink, and his round eyes never ceased watching, over the rim of the glass, Deliliers's perfect movements as he danced at a distance with young girls or with the smartest and most expensive-looking women. As soon as they returned from their drive, they both went punctually to put on evening dress; Fadigati's was grave and heavy and black, Deliliers wore a natty white jacket, short on the hips.

They went on the beach together too—although in the morning it was usually Fadigati who left the hotel first.

He arrived before nine o'clock, when there was still nobody about, greeted respectfully by the bathing hut assistants, whom (people said) he always tipped generously. He was dressed from head to foot in normal city clothes (only later, when it grew hotter, he left off his tie and shoes, but the white panama hat with its brim lowered over his glasses he never took off at all), and went to sit down under the solitary umbrella which he had ordered to be set farther ahead than the rest, only a few yards from the sea. Stretched out in a chaise-longue, his hands crossed behind his neck and a detective story open on his knees, he remained for a good two hours, doing nothing and looking at the sea.

Deliliers would come along at about eleven o'clock. With his lazy, animal walk, which the slight difficulty of walking in his wooden beach shoes made even more elegant, he would cross the space of burning sand between the bathing huts and the tents unhurriedly, almost naked. The white trunks which he was still tying at his left hip, the gold chain he wore round his neck, from which a medal of the Madonna hung just above his thorax, somehow accentuated his nakedness. And although, especially during the first days, he found it something of an effort to greet even me, when he saw me there beside our tent; although, as he made his way through the spaces between the tents and umbrellas he never failed to wrinkle his forehead with annoyance; yet it was hard to believe him, for it was obvious that he felt most people there, men as well as women, in their hearts admired him, and this he enjoyed a great deal.

Everyone admired him, men and women, there was no doubt about it at all. But Fadigati had to make up for the indulgence which Deliliers was shown on the beach at Riccione by people from Ferrara.

In the tent next to us that year was Signora Lavezzoli, wife of the lawyer. Today she seems nothing but an old woman and has lost much of her old importance. But then, in the mature splendour of her forty years, surrounded by the perpetual deference of her three adolescent children, two boys and a girl, and the no less perpetual deference of her worthy husband, the distinguished expert in civil law, a university don and an ex-deputy, well, in those days she could be considered one of those who most authoritatively inspired public opinion in our town.

Pointing her eyeglasses at the umbrella Deliliers made for, Signora Lavezzoli, who was born and had grown up at Pisa, "on the banks of the Arno", and used her quick Tuscan speech with extraordinary dexterity, kept us continually informed of all that was happening over there.

With the tone of voice and almost the technique of a radio sports commentator, she would tell us how, say, the couple had got up and were now going to the nearest raft: obviously Deliliers had expressed a wish to go bathing and the "old man", so as not to wait "palpitating" under the umbrella, had got permission to go with him. Or else she would describe Deliliers' gymnastics after bathing to dry himself off in the sun, while the "beloved" stood there doing nothing with a sponge towel in his hand, so anxious to dry him and touch him, she'd swear.

Oh, that Deliliers—she would then comment from her tent to ours, though addressing my mother in particular: believing she had lowered her voice, perhaps, so as not to let the children hear, but in fact talking louder than ever—that Deliliers was nothing but a spoilt boy, a lout that military service would do a great deal of good. But Dr. Fadigati, no. A man of his class, of his age, was in no way excusable. Well, so he had special tastes? He was "like that"?

What of it! No one had ever made a fuss of it before. But to come and make an exhibition of himself here at Riccioni, where of course he knew people would know him; to come and make a spectacle of himself here, while everywhere in Italy there were thousands of beaches where there would be absolutely no danger of meeting a single person from Ferrara! No, really: only someone really filthy (and as she said this Signora Lavezzoli's big blue eyes would shoot great flames of authentic indignation) only a "real degenerate"—she went on—would do a thing like that.

Signora Lavezzoli went on talking, and I would have given a great deal to shut her up once and for all. I felt she was unjust. I didn't like Fadigati, of course, but it wasn't he who seemed offensive. I knew Deliliers's character perfectly well. In choosing this beach so near to Ferrara, he had shown all his beastliness, all his lack of restraint. Fadigati had had nothing to do with it, I was sure. My feeling was, he felt ashamed. If he didn't greet me, if he even pretended not to recognize me, that must be why.

Unlike Lavezzoli, who had been at the sea since the beginning of August and so like everyone else knew all about the scandal (though while his wife held court all he did was read *Anthony Adverse* in his tent; I never even heard him speak), my father arrived at Riccione only on the morning of the 25th, a Saturday: even later than he had expected to be, and not knowing a thing, of course. He came by train without warning, and not finding a soul at home, even the cook, came down to the beach at once.

He noticed Fadigati almost at once. And before my mother or the Lavezzolis could stop him he went gaily across to him.

"Just look who's here!" he cried, striding up to the doctor's big umbrella.

Fadigati jerked round. My father was already holding out his hand, and Fadigati tried to pull himself up out of his chaise-longue.

At last he managed to. After which, for at least five minutes, we saw them standing under the big umbrella, talking with their backs to us.

Both of them were gazing at the motionless strip of sea, smooth, palely luminous, completely unruffled. And my father, whose whole person expressed the joy of having "shut up shop" (this was how he put it at Riccione when he wanted to refer to all the unpleasant things he had left in town: business, the empty house, the heat of summer, melancholy lunches at the *Roveraro*, mosquitoes, etc.), raised his arm and pointed out to Fadigati the hundreds of rafts scattered at odd distances along the shore, and, a long way off, scarcely visible on the horizon and as if suspended in mid-air, the rust-coloured sails of small fishing boats. At last they came towards our tent, Fadigati about a yard in front of my father with a strange expression on his face, at once imploring, disgusted, and guilty. It must have been eleven o'clock; Deliliers had not yet appeared. As I got up to meet them, I noticed the doctor glanced anxiously at the line of bathing huts, from where, at any minute, he hoped or feared to see his friend emerge.

9

He kissed my mother's hand.

"You do know Signor Lavezzoli, don't you?" my father said loudly, right away.

Fadigati hesitated a moment. He looked at my father, and nodded; then turned, obviously on tenterhooks, towards the Lavezzoli's tent.

Lavezzoli seemed more than ever immersed in *Anthony Adverse*. The three children lay on the sand a couple of yards away, in a ring round a blue towel, browning their backs, as immobile as lizards. Their mother was embroidering a tablecloth, which hung in long folds from her knees. She looked like a Renaissance madonna on a throne of clouds.

My father, who was famous for his straightforwardness, had noticed nothing amiss in the situation until he found himself up to his neck in it.

"Just look who's here!" he cried.

Before her husband could answer, Signora Lavezzoli intervened. She looked quickly up from her tablecloth, and suddenly held out the back of her hand to Fadigati.

"Of course, of course," she warbled, and smiled invitingly, showing her fine mouthful of teeth.

Downcast, Fadigati crossed over to the sun, walking a little unsteadily as usual because of wearing shoes on the sand. When he reached the Lavezzolis' tent, he kissed Signora Lavezzoli's hand, shook hands with her husband, who meantime had risen, and shook hands too with the three children, one by one. Finally he came back to our tent, where my father had already prepared a chaise-longue for him beside my mother. He seemed much calmer than a while before: relieved as a student after a difficult exam.

As soon as he was sitting down he gave a sigh of satisfaction.

"How lovely it is here," he said. "How delightfully airy!"

He turned sideways to talk to me.

"Remember last month at Bologna, how terribly hot it was?" he said.

Then he explained to my parents, whom I had never told anything about our meetings on the morning train at 6.50, how for the last three months we had been "the best of friends". He talked casually, like a man of the world. Obviously he could scarcely believe that he was there with us, even with the alarming Lavezzolis, restored to what just then he regarded as *his* circle, accepted again by the cultivated, well-bred society to which he had always belonged. "Ah!" he said every now and then, throwing out his chest for a breath of balmy sea air. It was clear that he felt free and happy: and at the same time filled with gratitude (a little indiscreetly, I thought) towards everyone who allowed him to feel so.

Meantime my father had started talking about the incredible sultriness of August in Ferrara.

"You couldn't sleep at night," he said, with a grimace of discomfort, as if the memory of the heat in the city was enough to make him feel its oppressiveness. "Do believe me, doctor, you couldn't sleep a wink. Some people say the modern age began in the year when Flit was invented. I don't dispute it. But Flit means you've got to have the windows hermetically sealed. And closed windows means sheets that stick to your skin with sweat. I'm not joking; till yesterday I swear I dreaded the coming of night. Those damned mosquitoes!"

"Here it's completely different," said Fadigati enthusiastically. "Even on the hottest nights you can always breathe."

And he began to dwell on the advantages of the Adriatic compared with the whole of the rest of Italy. He was Venetian, he admitted, he had spent his childhood and adolescence on the Lido, so probably his judgement was not entirely unbiased. But he did really feel the Adriatic was a great deal more restful than the Tyrrhenian.

Signora Lavezzoli pricked up her ears. Disguising her malice with a pretence at civic pride, she began defending the Tyrrhenian warmly. If, like him, she could have chosen between a holiday at Riccione and one at Viareggio, she wouldn't have hesitated a moment, she declared.

"Look at the way it is in the evenings," she continued. "Going past the café Zanarini makes you feel you're not a single mile from Ferrara. In the summer at least, it's rather nice, quite frankly, to see new faces: just once in a way different from those you see the rest of the year. It feels like walking along the Giovecca, or along the Corsa Roma, along the arches of the caffè della Borsa, don't you think so?"

Fadigati moved uneasily on his chaise-longue. Again his eyes crept across to the bathing huts. But there was still no sign of Deliliers.

"Perhaps, perhaps," he replied with a nervous smile, and looked out to sea again.

As happened every morning between eleven and twelve, the water had quickly changed colour. It was no longer the pale oily mass it had been half an hour before. The wind from the open sea, the sun which stood almost at its zenith, had made it smooth and blue, scattered with innumerable glints of gold. The first bathers began to run across the beach. And the three Lavezzoli children, when they had asked their mother's permission, went to their bathing hut to change.

"Perhaps," repeated Fadigati. "But, dear lady, where do you find afternoons like those the sun gives us here, when it sets behind 'the blue vision of San Marino'?"

He declaimed Pascoli's line in a sing-song, slightly nasal voice, separating each syllable and accentuating the diaeresis in *vision*. An embarrassed silence followed, but the doctor went on at once.

"I know of course that the sunsets on the Levant Riviera are magnificent. All the same, you have to pay dearly for them: the price, I mean, is burning hot afternoons, with the sea turned into a kind of burning-glass, so that people have to shut themselves up at home or at best to take refuge in the pine-woods. You will have noticed, too, the colour of the Adriatic after midday. It's more black than blue, it never dazzles one. The surface of the water doesn't reflect the sun's rays, it absorbs them. Or rather it does reflect them, but in the direction of . . . Yugoslavia! As for me," he continued, as if he had forgotten nothing, "I always long for lunch to be over so that I can come back to the beach at once. There's no lovelier moment to enjoy our divine Amarissimo in perfect peace than two in the afternoon."

"I imagine you come here with your . . . inseparable friend," said Signora Lavezzoli acidly.

Called rudely back to reality, Fadigati was silent and confused. Then, several hundred yards away, in the direction of Rimini, a crowd suddenly gathering attracted my father's attention.

"What's happening?" he asked, putting a hand to his forehead to see better.

Shouts of hurrah and clapping came to us on the wind.

"It's the Duce going into the water," explained Signora Lavezzoli reproachfully.

My father made a face. "Surely they don't cheer him even in the sea?" he growled between his teeth.

Romantic, patriotic, politically ingenuous and inexperienced like so many other Jews of his generation, my father had joined the fascist party when he returned from the front in 1919. So he had been a fascist from the very beginning and this in his heart he had remained, in spite of his mildness and integrity. But since Mussolini, after his early quarrels, had begun to make friends with Hitler, he had grown anxious. He thought of nothing but a possible outburst of antisemitism in Italy too, and every now and then, though suffering for it, he let fall some bitter comment on the régime.

"He's so simple, so human," went on Signora Lavezzoli, taking no notice of him. "Such a good husband, too. Every Saturday morning he takes the car and dashes off, and he's quite capable of coming all the way from Rome to Riccione in one go."

"Marvellous!" sneered my father. "How happy Donna Rachele must be!"

He looked meaningly at Lavezzoli, trying to get him to agree. Lavezzoli was no fascist. He had even signed Croce's famous Manifesto in 1924 and for some years, at least until 1930, he was supposed to be a Liberal democrat and antifascist. It was all in vain, though. Lavezzoli's eyes had at last been torn from the closely printed pages of *Anthony Adverse*, but were insensible to my father's silent pleading. Stretching out his neck, half-closing his eyes, he was staring obstinately at the water. The children had hired a boat and were going too far into the open sea. . .

"The other day," said Signora Lavezzoli, "Filippo

and I were going home arm-in-arm through the Viale dei Mille. It was half-past seven or a little later. Suddenly, through the gate of a house, who d'you think I saw coming? The Duce himself, dressed in white from head to foot. Instinctively I said 'Good evening, your Excellency.' And he took off his hat and said most charmingly: 'Good evening, madam.' Isn't it true, Pippo," she went on, turning to her husband, "isn't it true he was terribly nice?" Lavezzoli nodded.

"Perhaps we should be modest enough to recognize we were mistaken," he said gravely, turning to my father. "We mustn't forget it was he who gave us our Empire."

I can remember every word spoken that far-away morning, as if everything was taken down on a tape recorder.

When he had pronounced sentence (my father's eyes opened wide as he heard it), Lavezzoli returned to his book. But there was no stopping his wife. Encouraged by what her husband had said, and in particular by the word *Empire*, which she had probably never yet heard on her husband's austere lips, she continued to insist on the Duce's good heart and on the generous nature he had inherited from his birthplace, the Romagna.

"That reminds me," she said. "I must tell you

something I saw for myself three years ago right here at Riccione. One morning the Duce was bathing with the eldest boys, Vittorio and Bruno. About one o'clock he came out of the water and what d'you think was waiting for him? A telegram had arrived a moment before with the news of the assassination of the Austrian Chancellor Dollfuss. That year our tent was very close to the Mussolinis' tent, so what I'm saying is really true. As soon as he read the telegram, the Duce came out with a tremendous swear word in dialect—oh, of course, one must realize he's a passionate man! Then he began crying, I saw the tears running down his cheeks! They were great friends, the Mussolinis and the Dollfusses. What's more, Dollfuss's wife, a tiny, thin, very pretty, unobtrusive little creature, was their guest that very summer with the children. And as he wept the Duce was obviously thinking of what he'd have to say in a few minutes to that unhappy mother, when they all got together for lunch. . . ."

Suddenly Fadigati rose to his feet. Since Signora Lavezzoli's poisonous remarks had wounded him so deeply, he had not opened his mouth. All he did was bite his lips thoughtfully. Why was Deliliers so long? What could have happened?

"Will you excuse me?" he stammered, embarrassed.

"But it's early," protested Signora Lavezzoli. "Aren't you waiting for your friend? There are still twenty minutes to go!"

Fadigati stammered something incomprehensible. He shook hands all round and then went off in the direction of his umbrella. When he reached it he leant down to pick up the detective story and the sponge towel, and then we saw him cross the beach under the midday sun, but this time going directly to the hotel.

He walked tiredly, holding his detective story under his arm and the towel over his shoulder, his face altered with sweat and with anxiety. So much so that my father, who had been told everything right away, and was following his progress with pitying eyes, murmured softly: "Poor chap."

10

Straight after lunch I went back to the beach alone.

I sat in our tent. Yes, at two in the afternoon the Adriatic became dark blue, almost black. That day, though, as far as you could see, the top of every wave was crested with a tuft of foam, whiter than snow. The wind was still blowing from the open sea, but now came a little sidelong. If I raised my father's military field-glasses to take in the spur of the Punta di Pesaro which closed in the arc of the bay on my right, I could see high up the tops of the pines doubled over, and their foliage flung wildly about. Pressed on by the afternoon wind from Greece the long, ink-coloured, white-crested waves came on in serried and successive ranks. From where I was, they seemed to be hurling themselves to land like an invasion force. But, as they approached, their foamy crests gradually diminished, and vanished altogether in the last few yards. Stretched out on my chaise-longue, I could hear the dull roar of each wave against the shore.

The empty sea, from which the fishermen's sails had gradually disappeared (on the following morning, which was Sunday, I would see most of them spread out on the benches of the canal gates at Rimini and Cesenatico), was like the empty beach. In a tent not far from ours someone was playing a gramophone. I couldn't say what music it was, perhaps it was jazz. For more than three hours I stayed so, my eyes fixed on an old cockleshell fisherman dragging the bottom of the sea not far from the shore, and my ears filled with that music, which was no less sad and tireless than he was. When I got up, shortly after five, the old man was still searching, the gramophone still playing. The sun was setting and the shadows of the tents and the umbrellas had lengthened. The shadow of Fadigati's umbrella now nearly touched the water.

Outside the Grand Hotel, facing the sea, was a pavilion adjoining the beach. As soon as I set foot there, I noticed Fadigati sitting on one of the cement benches in front of the outside staircase of the hotel.

He had seen me too. Too late to avoid him!

"Good afternoon," I said, and went up to him.

He indicated the bench. "Why don't you sit down? Do, for a moment."

I obeyed. He put his hand into the inside pocket of his jacket, took out a packet of Nazionali cigarettes, and offered them to me. There were only two cigarettes in the packet. He realized I was hesitating to accept.

"They're Nazionali!" he exclaimed, a strangely fanatical gleam in his eyes.

At last he realized the reason for my hesitation and smiled.

"Oh go on, do take one!" he said. "We'll share them like good friends, one for you and one for me."

A car whistled on the asphalt and curved into the square. Fadigati turned to look at it, but without hope. And it wasn't his Alfa: it was a Fiat 1500, a grey Berlin.

"I think I should go," I said. All the same I took one of the two cigarettes.

He noticed my beach shoes. "I see you've come from the beach. The sea must have been wonderful today."

"Yes, but not for swimming," I said.

"Don't ever think of bathing before the right time, I do beg you!" he exclaimed. "You're a boy and of course your heart's excellent, you lucky fellow, but congestion may strike in a moment, even the strongest."

He held out the lighted match to me. "And now, have you got a date?" he asked.

I answered—and it was quite true—that at six the young Lavezzolis were expecting me. We had arranged to meet on the tennis court behind the café Zanarini. It was true it was still twenty to six. But I had to go home and change and get my racket and balls; in fact I was afraid I wouldn't be in time.

"Let's hope Fanny doesn't get it into her head to come too!" I went on. "Mummy won't let her come without doing her pigtails, and that'll mean I'll lose another good ten minutes."

While I was talking, I saw him carry out a curious ritual. He took the Nazionali from his lips so as to light it at the opposite end, where the trade mark was. Then he threw away the empty packet. Only then did I realize that the ground around us was scattered with cigarette stubs, more than a dozen.

"Have you seen how much I smoke?" he said.

"I have."

A question was burning on my lips: "What about Deliliers?" But I couldn't bring it out.

I got up and shook hands.

"Before, if I'm not mistaken, you didn't smoke at all," I said.

"I'm trying to make my modest contribution to

the spread of sore throats," he retorted wretchedly. "I thought I ought to."

I moved off a few steps.

"Did you say the tennis court near the café Zanarini?" he called after me. "Maybe later I'll come along and admire you."

Afterwards we learnt that nothing serious had happened to Deliliers. Just this: instead of bathing at Riccione, he had suddenly got it into his head to bathe at Rimini, where, high up in the Hotel Vittoria, he knew some sisters from Parma. He had taken the car and vanished without even bothering to leave a note for Fadigati, and came back about eight o'clock, Signora Lavezzoli told us, when she happened to be drinking an aperitif with her husband in the hall of the Grand Hotel. Suddenly they had seen Deliliers crossing the hall in a great hurry, looking furiously angry, with Fadigati almost in tears at his heels.

It was Deliliers who came up to me that same evening on the terrace of the Grand Hotel.

I had gone there with my parents and the Lavezzolis again, the lawyer and his wife. I was still tired from the tennis, and so not dancing, but listening in silence to Signora Lavezzoli, who, though clearly she must have known how much it would wound us, had begun talking "objectively" of Hitler's Germany

—just imagine!—and its "undeniable" greatness.

"You must realize, though, that your dear Dollfuss appears to have been liquidated by Hitler," I tried to make her see.

"What does that mean?" she retorted at once, with the compassionate and patient air of a schoolmistress ready to justify any amount of cheating in her brightest pupil. "That's political necessity, alas. Let's leave our personal likes or dislikes out of it: the fact is that in certain circumstances the head of a government, a statesman worthy of the name, must for the good of his own people pass over the sensibilities of ordinary people . . . little people like ourselves." And she smiled proudly, completely contradicting her last words.

Horrified, my father opened his mouth to say something. But once again Signora Lavezzoli gave him no time. As if she was changing the subject, she turned directly to him, and went on to describe an "interesting" article which had appeared in the last number of *Catholic Civilization*, signed by the well-known Father Gemelli.

The theme of the article was the so-called Jewish question. According to Father Gemelli, she said, the recurrent persecutions of the "Israelites" in every part of the world for nearly two thousand years could only be explained as a sign of God's anger.

The article ended with this question: May a Christian, even if in his heart he hates the idea of violence, pass judgement on historical events through which God's will is expressed?

At that point, not very politely, I got up from my cane armchair and left.

And so I was leaning against the side of the large window that separated the dining-room from the terrace, and the orchestra, if I am not mistaken, had started *Blue Moon.*

> *But you, pale moon, why*
> *Are you so sad, what is . . .*

the usual idiotic voice was singing, when suddenly I felt two fingers tapping me hard on the shoulder.

"Hello," said Deliliers.

It was the first time he had spoken to me at Riccione. "Hello," I answered. "How are you?"

"A bit better today," he said, winking. "What about you? What are you doing?"

"Oh reading, working," I lied. "I've got a couple of exams in October."

"Oh of course!" said Deliliers, thoughtfully scratching his hair, that shone with brilliantine, with his little finger.

But he wasn't thinking about his hair. Suddenly his expression changed. In a low voice, as if letting me into an important secret, peering back over his shoulder every now and then as if he were afraid of being surprised, he quickly told me about his bathe at Rimini with the two girls from Parma.

"Why don't you come with me tomorrow morning in the car? I'm going back. Come on, do help me! I can't go with two girls all on my own. Just leave your old work!"

At the end of the room Fadigati appeared, wearing a dinner jacket, his short-sighted eyes peering round behind his spectacles. The moonlit gloom created artificially for *Blue Moon* prevented him seeing Delilier's white jacket straight away.

"Well," I said, "I don't know if I can."

"I'll wait for you in the hotel."

"I'll try and come. What time do we leave?"

"Half-past nine. That all right?"

"Yes, but it's not definite."

I jerked my chin in Fadigati's direction. "You're wanted."

"Well, that's fixed then?" said Deliliers, turning on his heel and going up to Fadigati who was feverishly cleaning his spectacles with his handkerchief.

And a few seconds later the unmistakable roar of the Alfa-Romeo rose from the nearby square to tell the entire hotel that the "couple", perhaps to celebrate their reconciliation, had decided to make it a very special evening.

11

I must confess that the following morning I was tempted for a moment to go to Rimini with Deliliers.

What attracted me most was the thought of going along the sea road by car. But afterwards?—I wondered. What did Deliliers's suggestion really mean? And who really were these sisters from Parma he had told me about? Were they two ordinary girls we could take into the pine-woods, which was all too easy; or two girls of good family we must entertain on the beach under the sharp eyes of another Signora Lavezzoli? In either case (though it wasn't quite out of the question that they might come somewhere between the two!) I didn't feel I was friendly enough with Deliliers to accept his invitation light-heartedly. If I accepted, I foresaw a day full of regrets and humiliations; and besides, why ever had Deliliers, who had never really liked me or shown any sort of regard for me, suddenly asked me, almost implored me, to go "womanizing" with him? Was it perhaps because he wanted to show me that it wasn't a matter of vice, his being with Fadigati, but just to have his holiday paid for, and that in any case he always preferred a pretty girl?

In the end I stayed behind. And when, a little later, I saw Fadigati on the beach under his big umbrella, abandoned in a solitude that suddenly appeared to me immense and incurable, I felt, deep within me, repaid for what I had given up. I at least had not deceived him, I thought; when I was asked to join someone who was deceiving him and taking advantage of him, I had managed to resist, and kept a minimum of respect for him.

Then I thought he might like a little company.

A moment before I reached his umbrella he turned.

"Oh it's you," he said, but without surprise. "How nice of you to come and see me."

Everything about him showed the weariness and the suffering caused by a recent quarrel. Although very likely he had dragged a promise to stay from Deliliers, the boy had gone to Rimini just the same.

Fadigati shut the book he was reading and laid it down on a stool there beside him, half in shadow and half in the sun. It was not the usual detective story, but a small volume with an old flowered paper cover.

"What were you reading?" I asked, with a gesture at the book. "Is it poetry?"

"Have a look."

It was a school edition of the first canto of the *Iliad*, translated line by line.

"I found it in my suitcase," he said. "Mènin aèide teà peleiadeo Achillèos," he added, with a bitter smile.

My parents arrived just then, my mother holding Fanny's hand. I waved to show them where I was, and whistled the family signature tune: the first line of a Schubert *Lied*.

Fadigati turned, half-rose from his chaise-longue, and raised his panama hat politely. My parents answered together: my mother nodding slightly, my father touching the visor of his brand-new white cloth cap with two fingers. I realized at once that they disliked seeing me with Fadigati. As soon as she saw me, Fanny had turned to ask my mother something, probably permission to join me. But clearly my mother had stopped her.

"How very sweet your sister is," said Fadigati. "How old is she?"

"Twelve: exactly eight years younger than me," I answered, embarrassed.

"But there are three of you altogether, I believe," he said.

"Yes, there are. Two boys and a girl: there are

four years between each of us. Ernesto, the second, is in England. . . ."

"What an intelligent little face!" said Fadigati, still looking in Fanny's direction. "And how well that pink bathing dress suits her! She's lucky to have two big brothers, you know."

"Oh, she's still a kid," I said.

"Oh yes, so I see. I'd have thought she was ten or so. But that means nothing. Girls develop all of a sudden. You'll have such a surprise. . . . She's at high school, isn't she?"

"Yes, in the third form."

He shook his head with a kind of melancholy regret, as if he were thinking of all the effort and the pain which every human being must meet to grow, to come to maturity. But his thoughts soon changed.

"And what about Signora Lavezzoli?" he asked.

"Oh, her. I think this morning, because of Mass, we shan't see them before midday."

"Oh that's true, today's Sunday," he said, startled. "Well, in that case," he added, after another pause, as he got to his feet, "let's go and say how d'you do to your parents."

We walked side by side along the sand, already uncomfortably hot.

"I've a feeling," he said to me, "I've a feeling Signora Lavezzoli doesn't like me all that much."

"Oh no, I don't think so."

"All the same, it's not a bad idea to take advantage of her absence."

Without the Lavezzolis, my parents were unable to stick to their obvious resolution to keep him at a distance: especially my father, who was soon talking to him in the friendliest way.

A light wind was coming up from inland, the wind called the *garbino*. The sea had no sails at all on it, and though the sun had not yet reached its zenith, it already looked dark: a thick, leaden colour. Perhaps because he had just read the first canto of the *Iliad*, Fadigati spoke of the Greeks' feeling for nature, and in particular of the meaning he thought we must attribute to adjectives like *purple* and *violet*, applied by Homer to the sea. My father then spoke of Horace, and of Carducci's *Odi Barbare* which he considered—and we argued over it almost daily— his ideal in the field of modern poetry. In fact they chatted so agreeably (the fact that Deliliers was not likely to pop out from the bathing huts from one minute to the next obviously steadied the doctor's nerves), that when the Lavezzoli family, fresh from Mass, landed on us complete towards midday, Fadigati felt strong enough, protected enough, so to speak, to bear Signora Lavezzoli's inevitable remarks quite casually, and even to answer back quite successfully.

We saw no more of Deliliers on the beach: neither that day nor the days that followed. He never returned from his sorties in the car before two o'clock in the morning and Fadigati, left on his own, sought our company more than ever.

And so it was that, apart from spending the morning in our tent (it hardly seemed true to my father that he could discuss music, literature and art with him, instead of politics with Signora Lavezzoli!), he got into the habit of coming to the tennis court behind the café Zanarini in the afternoon when he heard that the Lavezzoli children and I were going there.

There was certainly nothing very exciting about our lazy games, one male couple against one mixed couple. I was a pretty poor player, but Franco and Gilberto Lavezzoli could hardly hold a racket. And as for Cristina, their blonde, rosy and delicate sister of fifteen (she emerged from a convent boarding school in Florence every now and then, and had the entire family running round her), she played even worse than her brothers. Her hair grew in a little crown round her head—"like one of Melozzo's singing angels", as Fadigati put it, with fatherly admiration, one day—and rather than disarrange a single curl she would have given up walking. So there was absolutely no question of her bothering about the style of a drive or having a decent backhand!

Yet in spite of all this, Fadigati seemed to be highly interested in our game, however boring and pointless it was.

"Good shot!" "Only just out!" "Bad luck!" He was generous with his praise for all of us, and had some comment, sometimes wildly out, for every shot.

Sometimes our game languished a bit too much even for such an indulgent audience.

"Why don't you play a match?" he would suggest.

"Oh dear," Cristina would protest at once, blushing. "I just can't handle a ball!"

But he refused to listen.

"Order of the Day!" he proclaimed gaily. "Doctor Fadigati will give the winning couple a prize of two superb bottles of San Pellegrino orangeade!"

He ran to the keeper's hut and dragged out a rickety and dangerous umpire's chair at least two yards high, pulled it to one side of the tennis court himself and finally clambered up it. Gradually the air darkened; his hat appeared in the half-light aureoled by a cloud of flies. But, perched up there like a great bird, he stayed and called out the score in a metallic voice, determined to keep up his role as an impartial umpire to the end. Obviously he had no idea what else to do, or how to fill the terrible emptiness of the days.

12

As often happens on the Adriatic, at the beginning of September the weather suddenly changed. It rained only one day, August 31st, but the fine weather on the following day fooled nobody. The sea was unquiet and green, a vegetable green; the sky exaggeratedly transparent, jewel-like. In the very warmth of the air pricked a tiny persistent hint of cold.

At once the number of holiday-makers decreased. On the beach the three or four rows of tents and umbrellas were quickly reduced to two, and then, after another day of rain, to one. Even the bathing huts of the various hotels began gradually to be taken down. Looking backwards, you could see far across the dunes, which until a few days ago were covered with scorched, stunted brushwood, and where now miraculously bloomed incredible numbers of wonderful yellow flowers, as tall as lilies.

To anyone who knew that part of the coast it was clear what they meant: the summer was now over; from then onwards it would be nothing but a memory.

I took the chance of settling down to work. At least two exams in Ancient History were coming up the following October, so until about midday I stayed in my room reading the set books.

The same thing happened every afternoon, till it was time for tennis.

One day after lunch, while I was working (I hadn't even gone to the beach, that morning: as soon as I got up the distant roar of the sea had removed any notion I might have had of bathing), I heard Signora Lavezzoli's shrill voice rising from the garden, and, though unable to make out what she was saying, I understood from her tone that she was indignant about something.

"Oh no . . . last night's scandal . . ." I managed to catch.

What was the matter with her? Why had she come to see us? I wondered, annoyed. And suddenly, instinctively, I thought of Fadigati.

I resisted the temptation to go down and listen behind the door that gave on to the garden. An hour later, when I went down, Signora Lavezzoli had gone. My father was sitting in the shade of a pine-tree, as usual. As soon as he heard the sound of my footsteps on the gravel he looked up from his newspaper. I was dressed for tennis; in one hand I was holding the handlebars of my bicycle, in the other my racket. All the same he asked me:

"Where are you going?"

Two summers before, at Riccione, I had had a love affair with a woman of thirty from Milan, whom my mother knew slightly. I had only just taken school cert, and it was the first time that such a thing had happened to me. Not knowing whether to be proud of my adventure or worried about it, my father kept track of every move I made. I had only to get ready to leave the house or even the tent: and at once he gave me a look that was half-timid and half-inquiring.

Now I saw the identical expression in the look he gave me. I felt the blood mount to my head.

"Can't you see?" I said dryly.

He looked away from me. Apart from looking worried, he seemed tired. Signora Lavezzoli's visit, which I guessed was unexpected, had stopped him taking his usual afternoon nap.

"I don't think you'll find anyone there," he said. "Signora Lavezzoli was here a minute ago. She came to say her children won't be there today. The two boys have to study, and she wouldn't send Cristina alone."

I glanced at Fanny, who was squatting alone at the end of the garden with her doll. From the back, with her small shoulder-blades jutting up under her jersey, her pigtails bleached by the sun, she seemed even thinner and more immature than usual. My father pointed to the cane armchair in front of his.

"Sit down a minute," he said, and smiled uncertainly at me.

He meant to talk to me, but disliked doing so, that was obvious. I pretended not to have heard.

"It was nice of her to bother, but I'm going just the same," I said, turning round and going towards the gate.

"There's a letter from Ernesto," my father called plaintively after me. "Don't you even want to read it?"

Just by the gate I stopped, and at that moment Fanny looked up. From a distance she gave me a long look that seemed to indicate disapproval.

"Later, when I get back," I answered, and pedalled off.

Before I went into the tennis court enclosure, I saw Fadigati at once through the wire netting. He was standing by the umpire's chair which was still there from the previous afternoon, smoking, looking ahead of him.

He turned.

"Oh, you're alone," he said. "What about the others?"

I laid the bicycle against the wire netting and went up to him. "They aren't coming today," I answered.

He smiled feebly, crookedly; and at this point I realized that his upper lip was rather swollen and that one of the glasses of his smart gold-rimmed spectacles was cracked twice.

"I don't know why," I said, looking at him. "It seems that Franco and Gilberto have to study. But I know it's an excuse. All the same I hope . . ."

"I'll tell you why," Fadigati interrupted bitterly. "It's obviously because of what happened last night."

"What happened?"

"Don't tell me you don't know," he said, desperately. "Of course I didn't see you this morning on the beach. But can you possibly not have heard your parents speak of it later, say at table?"

I convinced him easily enough. Yes, I told him, I had heard Signora Lavezzoli say the word "scandal", and I explained how and when, but I knew nothing else.

Then, looking round again, he began telling me how the previous evening, in the hall of the Grand Hotel, "in front of everyone", he had had an "argument" with Deliliers.

"I was scolding him, but quietly of course, about

the way he's been carrying on just recently; always running round in the car . . . so much so that really I hardly see him at all. When suddenly, d'you know what he did? He got up and *Wham!*—he banged his fist right into my face!"

He touched his swollen lip.

"Here, d'you see?"

"Does it hurt?"

"Oh no," he said, shrugging. "It's true I fell flat and passed out. But after all, what does a blow mean? And even the scandal; what d'you think that means . . . compared with all the rest?"

He was silent. And I was silent too, filled with embarrassment. I thought of his words "compared with all the rest", as I saw before me the image of his suffering as a slighted lover, an image that, I must confess, made me feel revulsion rather than pity.

But that was only half of it.

"At one o'clock today, when I went back to the hotel from the beach," Fadigati continued, "the worst surprise was waiting for me. Look what I found up in our room."

From the pocket of his jacket he pulled out a folded piece of paper and handed it to me.

"Read it, do read it."

There was little to read, but it was quite enough. Printed in pencil I saw:

FROM ERALDO.

I folded the sheet in four and gave it back to him.

"He's gone . . . yes, he's gone," said Fadigati. "But the worst thing is," he added, his swollen lip trembling, his voice trembling too, "that he's taken everything with him."

"Everything!" I exclaimed.

"Yes. Apart from the car, which was his anyway, as I'd bought it specially for him, he took everything else: suits, linen, ties, two suitcases, a gold watch, a cheque book, a thousand lire which I had in the chest of drawers. He hasn't forgotten a single thing that belonged to me: not even my headed paper, not even my comb and toothbrush!"

He ended with a strange, almost exultant shout: as if, in a final count, the list of objects Deliliers had stolen had the effect of turning his distress into something stronger, something filled with pleasure and pride.

People were arriving: two young men and two girls, all four of them on bicycles.

"It's five forty five," one of the girls called gaily, consulting her wrist-watch. "We arranged to come at six, but as there's nobody playing couldn't we go ahead?"

Fadigati and I left the enclosure, and in silence

took the small acacia-lined road shut in between the red walls of the café Zanarini. In the courtyard beyond we could see the waiters crossing the paved dance floor, carrying chairs and tables.

"And what do you mean to do now?" I asked him.

"I'll leave tonight," said Fadigati. "There's a train leaving Rimini at nine that gets to Ferrara about half an hour after midnight. I hope I'll have enough left to pay the hotel bill."

I stared at him. He was wearing his town clothes, with his felt hat and everything. Well then, it's not true that Deliliers took everything, I thought, looking at his felt hat. He did exaggerate a bit!

"Why don't you go to the police?" I burst out coldly.

He stared at me. "Go to the police?" he muttered, surprised.

Suddenly his eyes flashed scornfully.

"Go to the police?" he repeated, and looked at me as one looks at a rather ridiculous stranger. "But d'you think I possibly could?"

13

We left Riccione on October 10th, a Saturday afternoon.

About the middle of the previous month the barometer settled at fine, and day followed splendid day, with cloudless skies and calm seas. But who cared? Who had the heart to notice it? What my father had feared so much was coming true. Less than a week after Fadigati left, all the Italian newspapers, chief among them the *Corriere Ferrarese*, started up the violent antisemitic campaign which after a year was to bring us to the racial laws of 1938.

I remember those first days like a nightmare: my father going brokenly out each morning in search of newspapers; my mother's eyes always swollen with tears; Fanny knowing nothing, yet somehow knowing it all; and my own unhappy longing to shut myself up in an obstinate silence. So as to avoid hearing Signora Lavezzoli discussing Christianity and Judaism as if nothing had happened, for instance how much we should blame the "Israelites" for the crucifixion of Jesus Christ (she highly disapproved of the government's new policy in regard to us, but all the same even the Pope had said in 1929, etc., etc.), so as to avoid all this, I had stopped appearing on the beach at all. I had quite enough and to spare listening to my father, who, in pointless discussions about the poisonous articles he kept reading, tried to enumerate the patriotic merits, or, come to that, the fascist merits, of the Jews in Italy. I too was desperate, though; but I forced myself to carry on preparing for my exam. I went for long solitary bicycle rides over the hills inland. Once, without telling anyone, with the result that when I returned I found my parents both in tears, I went as far as San Leo and into Carpegna, and was away altogether nearly three days. I thought endlessly of our return to town, thought of it with a kind of terror, with a feeling of intimate torment that kept growing and growing.

Finally it began raining again, and we had to leave.

As always happened when we returned from our holidays, as soon as I reached Ferrara I couldn't resist going on a trip round the city. I got the house porter to get out my old bicycle, and without setting foot in my room, or telephoning Vittorio Molon or Nino Bottecchiari, I went riding haphazardly off, without any precise end in view.

Towards evening I ended up on the Wall of the Angels, where I had spent so many afternoons as a child and an adolescent; and soon, pedalling along the path on the top of the bastion, I reached the Jewish cemetery.

Then I got off my bike and leant back against the trunk of a tree.

I looked round at the ground about me, where our people were buried. Among the few stones, that looked small in the distance, I could see a middle-aged man and woman, probably foreigners who had stopped between one train and the next, and had managed to get the necessary permission from Dr. Levi to visit the cemetery on the Sabbath. They wandered among the tombs as cautiously and remotely as guests or strangers. And then, as I looked at them and at the vast urban landscape spread out below me as far as I could see, I suddenly felt myself filled with great sweetness, with peace and tender gratitude. The setting sun, piercing a dark bank of clouds low on the horizon, lit everything vividly: the Jewish cemetery at my feet, the apse and campanile of the church of St. Christopher a little farther away, and in the distance, high above the dark extent of houses, the distant bulk of the castle and the cathedral. All I needed was to find the motherly face of my city unchanged, to have it all to myself once more, for that agonizing sense of exclusion that had tormented me in the last few days to fall away at once. The future of persecution and massacre that might await us (since I was a child I had continually heard of it as an eventuality that was always possible for us Jews) no longer frightened me.

And yet, who knows? I kept saying to myself as I turned homeward. Who can read the future?

My illusions were short-lived, though. The following morning, as I was walking under the porticoes of the café in Corso Roma, someone suddenly shouted my name.

It was Nino Bottecchiari. He was sitting alone at a table out of doors, and when he tried to get up nearly overturned his cup of coffee.

"Welcome back!" he exclaimed, coming up to me with his arms flung wide. "How long have we had the pleasure and honour of having you among us?"

When he heard I had been in Ferrara since five o'clock the previous day, he complained that I hadn't rung him up.

"Of course you'll say you were going to ring me today at lunchtime," he added, affectionately peeved. "Deny it if you can!"

I was going to telephone him, I was actually thinking of it when he called me; but for that very reason I was silent, confused.

"Come along and have some coffee with me," Nino went on, taking my arm, and trying to take me over to his table.

"Come home with me," I suggested.

"So early? It's not yet midday!" he replied. "Come along, now: you don't want to miss everyone coming out of Mass!"

He went ahead of me among the tables. I followed him, reluctantly, then suddenly stopped. Everything disturbed me, everything wounded me.

"Well, what's up?" said Nino, who was already sitting down.

"I've got to go, forgive me," I stammered, raising a hand to say good-bye.

"Wait!"

His shout, and the long manœuvres he was forced into to settle the bill (the old waiter Giovanni hadn't change for a fifty-lire note, and shambled off grumbling to change it at Barilari's, the nearby chemist), at once drew people's attention to Nino and me, and I felt I was being closely watched by a number of them. Even round the table of the fascist storm-troopers, at which that day, apart from the usual triumvirate consisting of Aretusi, Sturla, and Belli-

104

stracci, sat the Federal Secretary from Bologna, and Gino Cariani, secretary of the G.U.F., the talk, which till then had been fairly animated, suddenly stopped. After turning to stare at me, Cariani, servile as ever, leant over to whisper something in Aretusi's ear. I saw Sciagura make a face and nod gravely.

As I waited for Nino to get his change, I moved a few steps away. It was a beautiful day and Corso Roma seemed as gay and lively as ever. From under the portico of the café, across the pillars, I looked steadily at the centre of the street, where dozens of bicycles, ridden mostly by high-school boys, and glittering in the sun with chromium and colours, twirled in and out of the Sunday crowd. A fair boy of twelve or thirteen, still wearing short trousers, dashed by on a blue racing bike. He raised one arm and yelled "Hey!" I started and turned to see who it was; but he had already vanished round the corner of Giovecca.

And here at last was Nino.

"Sorry," he said breathlessly, "but one's got to be patient with that snail Giovanni."

We went off in the direction of the cathedral, walking side by side along the left-hand pavement.

They had been on holiday, as in other years, at Moena, in the valley of Fassa, Nino was saying meanwhile, telling me about himself and his family. Fields, fir-trees, cows, bells; the usual stuff, so usual that—and now he was sorry—he had thought it superfluous to send me the conventional postcard. Yes, he'd been pretty bored, he burst out. Luckily in August Uncle Mauro, the ex-socialist deputy, had come as their guest for a fortnight, and as soon as he got there he electrified the family atmosphere right away. And the pair of them together, uncle and nephew, had gone on some fine trips together.

"Oh yes, the old boy's still pretty bright, I can tell you," he told me, and winked. "What a character! He climbed mountains marvellously, singing the Red Flag at the top of his voice. In fact, we became friends; and he's even promised to take me into his office to get experience as soon as I've got my degree. . ."

We had now reached the main door of the Archbishop's palace.

"Let's go through here," suggested Nino, and went ahead of me into the cool dark entrance. At the end of it, the enclosed garden glowed stilly in the sunshine. And suddenly the noise of Corso Roma became a distant roar in which you could just make out the sound of bicycle bells.

Nino stopped.

"That reminds me," he said. "Have you heard about Deliliers?"

I felt oddly guilty all at once.

"Well, yes," I stammered absurdly. "I saw him at Riccione last month. We didn't go around together, though. I spoke to him once or twice. . . ."

"Oh I knew that!" Nino interrupted. "The news that he was at Riccione with that miserable Dr. Fadigati reached even Moena straight away. No, no, that's not what I meant."

And, giving me no time to recover from my embarrassment, he told me that a fortnight earlier he had had a letter from Deliliers—from Paris, no less! A pity he hadn't got it with him, he said, slapping the pockets of his jacket with his open palms. He would show it to me, though; it really was worth while. A document of such repulsive cynicism had never landed in his hands.

"How disgusting!" he exclaimed with energy. "D'you remember what he used to say? He said that some day he'd fix things up and then . . . and then take up boxing. Boxing, just imagine! He's already taken up with some other rich pansy, I can just see him doing it. If France wasn't the mess it is—and the fascists are right there—it wouldn't allow adventurers of that kind to stay. And as for us in Italy, d'you know what we ought to do to them? Shoot them, that's what, and have done with it. But d'you call this a society? I mean a society worthy of the

107

name? You should just hear the tone of his letter! He flings insults at us, says we're all mothers' boys, and provincial, and middle class . . . he takes it out on you, of course."

"What does he say?" I asked mechanically. "Calls me a dirty Jew, I suppose."

He hesitated before answering. In the half-light where we stood I saw him blushing.

"Come on, Mass will be over by now," he said, taking my arm.

And he dragged me almost by force towards the second exit of the Archbishop's palace: the one which, right on the corner of Via Gorgadello, gives out onto the cathedral square.

14

Twelve o'clock Mass was not yet over. As usual, though, a small crowd of boys and youths and idlers who belonged in the Piazza delle Erbe and in Corso Roma was getting into a semicircle round the cathedral precincts.

Until a few months before, I had never missed the half-past-twelve exit from San Carlo or the cathedral on a Sunday. And I was not to miss it even that day, after all. But today, I said to myself, today I was no longer down in the thick of it, laughing and joking about the one important and at the same time trivial topic: the coming procession of well-bred girls and their mothers. As I leant against the doorway of the Archbishop's palace, tucked away in a corner of the square (Nino's presence beside me increased my bitterness, if anything), I felt cut out, irrevocably an intruder.

The hoarse shout of a newsvendor echoed round just then.

It was Cenzo, a lame, squinting, almost half-witted creature of indefinable age who was always wandering about the pavements with a great bundle of newspapers under his arm. He was a fanatical supporter of the U.S. Estense, and very popular in town, and everyone, including myself, generally gave him good-natured slaps on the back and affectionate insults.

Dragging his old shoes along the pavement, Cenzo was going towards the middle of the square, in his right hand holding high an unfolded newspaper.

"Grand Council's impending measures against the Jews!" he yelled indifferently, in his hollow voice.

And while Nino stood silently, uneasily, beside me, I felt born in me, with unspeakable loathing, the Jew's ancient atavistic hatred for all that was Christian and Catholic: in fact, what was *goy*. I thought of Via Mazzini, of Via Vignatagliata, of the stunted street called Torcicorda: of the maze of narrow alleys, damp in winter and suffocating in summer, which had once made up the ghetto in Ferrara. *Goy*, *goîm*; how shameful, how humiliating, how disgusting to express myself so! Yet I managed to do it, like any east European Jew who had never lived outside the ghetto. In a more or less distant future, I was now certain they, the *goîm*, would force us to live there again, in the medieval district we had emerged from only seventy or eighty years ago. Heaped up behind the gates, like so many terrified beasts, we should never escape again.

"I didn't like talking to you about it," Nino began to say, without looking at me, "but you can't imagine how sorry I am about what's happening. My uncle, the M.P., is pessimistic about it, I can't hide it from you: but that's natural in him because he's *always* wanted things to go as badly as possible. But I just don't believe it. In spite of appearances I don't believe that Italy will behave like Germany towards you. You'll see the whole thing go up in smoke, like everything else."

I should have been grateful to Nino for bringing up the subject. What else could he have said? And yet I wasn't. While he was talking, I could scarcely hide the annoyance I felt at his words and at his tone in particular, the disappointed tone of his voice. "The whole thing will go up in smoke, like everything else," he had said. Could anything be more clumsy, more insensitive, more obtusely *goîm* than that?

I asked him why, unlike his uncle, he was so optimistic.

"Oh, we Italians are much too light-hearted," he

replied, without showing he had noticed my sarcasm. "We may imitate some things about the Germans, even the goose-step, but not their tragic sense of life. We're too old, believe me, too sceptical, too burnt out!"

It was only at this point that my silence made him notice the inopportuneness, the inevitable ambiguity of what he was saying. Suddenly his expression changed.

"It's better, don't you think?" he exclaimed with forced gaiety. "Long live our age-old Latin wisdom, after all!"

He was certain, he repeated, that anti-semitism would never take hold among us. All you had to do was think of Ferrara—and so many other Italian cities must be like it, socially speaking—to realize that a complete separation of the "Jewish element" from the "so-called Aryan element" was in practice quite unrealizable. The "Israelites" all, or nearly all, belonged to the most distinguished upper middle classes; in fact in a sense they were the most important part of it, its spinal column. The very fact that most of them had been fascists, many from the very beginning, showed their perfect solidarity and fusion with the climate around them. Could you imagine anyone more Jewish, and at the same time more from Ferrara, than the lawyer Geremia Tabet, just to take the first name that came into his head, who belonged to the few (among them Carlo Aretusi, Vezio Sturla, Osvaldo Bellistracci, the consul Bolognesi, and two or three others) who in 1919 founded the first local section of Fighting Fascists? Could anyone possibly be more one of "us" than old Dr. Corcos, Elia Corcos the famous surgeon, who was so much part of the town that he could perfectly well be incorporated in the municipal arms? And what about my father? And what about Bruno's father, the lawyer Lattes? No, no! You need only run through the telephone directory, where Jewish names invariably had professional and academic qualifications, to see at once that a policy of racial discrimination at Ferrara couldn't possibly have the smallest hope of being taken seriously. That sort of thing could succeed only if families like the Finzi-Continis, with their rather "typical" way of keeping themselves to themselves in a grand old mansion, and hardly being in touch with anyone (he himself knew Alberto Finzi-Contini fairly well, but had never once managed to set foot in their splendid private tennis court!) were more numerous. Whereas the Finzi-Continis were an exception in Ferrara, that was the point. And besides, mightn't they be simply following on in the historical tradition of some ancient aristocratic family, now extinct, whose palace in Corso Ercole I and land they now owned, as well as the system of living in isolation?

All this he said, and more, that I cannot remember. While he spoke, I looked away from him. The sky above the square was full of light; when I watched the doves flying across it now and then, I had to half-shut my dazzled eyes.

Suddenly he laid a hand on my arm.

"I wish you'd advise me," he said. "Advise me as a friend."

"What's it about?"

"Promise you'll be really honest?"

"Well, of course."

Some days before, he told me, he was approached by "that snake" Gino Cariani, who had suggested straight off that he should accept the post of fascist cultural organizer. His first impulse had been to refuse. But later, thinking it over. . . That same morning, in the café, a little before I arrived, Cariani had brought up the subject again.

"What should I do?" he asked at this point, after a pause.

His lips tightened with perplexity; I was silent. Then he went on talking.

"You know my family's traditions," he said. "All the same, you can be quite sure of this: when my father comes to hear I haven't accepted Cariani's

114

offer he'll literally tear his hair out, that's what he'll do. And as for my uncle, the M.P., d'you think he'll behave any differently? All Dad would have to do would be to ask him to send for me, and he'd do it right away, if only to make himself look completely unprejudiced. I can just see his face as he good-naturedly asks me to go back on my decision. I can already hear what he'll say. He'll tell me not to behave like a child, to reflect, because in Life, you know, etc., etc."

He laughed disgustedly.

"Look," he went on. "I've such a low opinion of human nature, and of the Italian character in particular, that I can't even be sure of myself. We live in a country, my dear chap, where all that's left of the Romans, the Romans in the old sense, is the raised-arm salute. Now I wonder: *à quoi bon?* When you get down to it, if I refused. . . ."

"You'd be wrong," I interrupted him calmly.

He stared at me, faintly suspicious.

"D'you really mean that?"

"Of course I do. I don't see why you shouldn't try and make a career in the Party or through the Party. If I were in your shoes . . . I mean, if I was studying law like you . . . I shouldn't hesitate a moment."

I was careful to let none of what I was feeling show. Nino's face cleared. He lit a cigarette: my objectivity, and my disinterestedness, had struck him profoundly.

He thanked me for my advice, blowing out a big mouthful of smoke. As for following it, though, he'd think it over during the next few days. He wanted to see things clearly and see clearly into himself. Fascism was in a crisis, there was no doubt about that. But was it a matter of a crisis *in* the system or *of* the system? Action was all very well: but how? To try and change things *from the inside*, or else. . .

He ended with a vague gesture of his hand.

All the same, he went on, during the next few days he'd come and see me at home. I was a literary man, it's true, he said, "a poet"—and he smiled, still trying to assume the old half-affectionate and half-protective politician's tone he often put on for my benefit. In any case he very much wanted to go over the whole business with me. We must ring each other up, meet, whatever happened keep in touch: in short, "react"!

"That reminds me," he asked suddenly, frowning. "When do you have your first exam in Bologna? Have to think of renewing our season tickets, dammit. . ."

15

I saw Fadigati again.

It was in the street at night: a damp, cloudy night the following November, on All Souls' Day. I was coming out of a brothel in Via Bomporto, feeling my clothes were steeped in the usual disgusting smell, and lingering there by the door unable to make up my mind to go home right away and longing to get up on the nearby city wall for a bit of fresh air.

There was perfect silence around me. From inside the brothel, behind me, came a weary conversation between three: two men and a woman. They were talking of sport: of football. The two men were deploring the fact that the U.S. Estense team, which had been such a grand team in the years immediately after the first world war, one of the strongest in northern Italy (in 1923, in fact, it had only just missed the championship of the First Division; all it needed was to win the last game), had now gone down and down to Series C and each year had to struggle every year to stay there at all. Oh the years when Condorelli was centre attack, when the two Banfis were playing, Beppe and Ilario, and the great Baùsi: those were the days! The woman spoke only occasionally, saying things like "Oh get along with you, you folk in Ferrara are much too fond of love," or else "It's not just getting into bed that ruins you, it's what you do when you get there!"

When they heard her the two men stopped talking for a moment as if they were thinking it over; then continued with the same subject. They must have been elderly men, about forty-five or fifty: old smokers. The woman was not from Ferrara, though. Perhaps she came from Venice, perhaps from Friuli.

Slowly, tripping over the sharp cobblestones in the alley, came heavy footsteps.

"But what is it you want? Are you hungry?"

The fog was so thick that I heard Fadigati's voice before I saw him.

"Stupid, dirty old thing," he continued in the same tone of kindly grumbling. "I've nothing to give you, you know!"

Who could he be talking to?

In the end he appeared. Aureoled by the yellow light of the only street lamp, his stout form showed up suddenly in the fog. He came forward slowly, bending slightly sideways, still talking: he was bending over a dog, I realized at once.

A few yards away from me he stopped.

"Well now, are you going to leave me in peace or not?"

He was staring into the dog's eyes, his first finger raised threateningly. And the dog, who was a mongrel bitch, white with brown spots (the result of a cross between a setter and a fox-terrier, probably), gazed up at him from below, wagging her tail desperately, damply, tremulously, and dragged herself across the cobblestones, towards the doctor's feet. In a moment she would have flung herself on her back, belly and legs in the air, completely at his mercy.

"Good evening."

He looked up at me from the dog.

"How are you?" he said, recognizing me at once. "Are you well?"

We shook hands. We were facing each other before the nailed front door of the brothel. My god, how old he'd grown! His pendulous cheeks, darkened by a bristly grey beard, made him look seventy. From his bleary red eyelids I could see that he was tired, that he slept very little. And yet, behind his spectacles, his glance was still alive and vigorous. . . .

"D'you know you've got thinner? But it suits

you, yes, it really suits you! It makes you much more grown up," he said. "You know sometimes in life it's just a few months that count. Those few months are sometimes more important than whole years."

The nailed door opened and four or five youths came out: they looked as if they were up from the suburbs, if not from the country. They waited a moment in a circle to light their cigarettes, and one of them went up to the wall beside the entrance and urinated. Meantime they all looked at us with strange insistence. (But weren't they right, after all? What were we up to, that old gentleman and I, there at that hour?)

A small stream wound quickly down to the centre of the alley under the open legs of the youth standing still against the wall. It attracted the dog, who cautiously went up and sniffed at it.

"We'd better go," whispered Fadigati, his voice trembling slightly.

We left in silence, while behind us the alley-way resounded suddenly with oaths and laughter. For a moment I feared that the small group would follow us. But then luckily we turned into Via Ripagrande, where the fog seemed even thicker.

All we had to do was cross the street and mount the opposite pavement; and I was certain right away that they had lost all trace of us.

We walked along side by side, more slowly, towards the Montagnone. Midnight had struck some time ago, and we met no one in the street. There were rows and rows of closed blind shutters, and shut doors: and, at intervals, the almost subaqueous lamplight.

It was so late that perhaps we two, Fadigati and I, were the only people still wandering about at that hour. He talked to me, heart-broken, submissive. He told me his troubles. They had got rid of him at the hospital, with some excuse. Apart from that, there were whole afternoons at his surgery in Via Gorgadello when not a single patient turned up. He had no one in the world, of course; he still had no immediate financial worries. But was it possible to go on living like this for long, in the most absolute solitude, surrounded by general hostility? Soon he would have to dismiss the nurse, get down to a smaller surgery, start selling his pictures. Better to go away at once, try and move somewhere else.

"Then why don't you?"

"You're quite right, of course," he sighed. "But at my age. . . And then, even if I had the courage and strength to decide on such a step, d'you think it would be any use?"

We had got near the Montagnone, when we heard a light padding behind us. We turned. It was the mongrel bitch again, trailing breathlessly after us.

She stopped, happy to have tracked us by her nose in that sea of fog. And flinging her long soft ears back on her neck, delightedly whining and wagging her tail, she renewed—in Fadigati's honour, especially—her pathetic protests of devotion.

"Is she yours?" I asked him.

"I should think not. I found her this evening, near the Aqueduct. I gave her a little pat, but she took me much too seriously, dammit. Since then I haven't been able to get rid of her."

I noticed her paps were big and hung down swollen with milk.

"She's got puppies, don't you see?"

"That's true!" exclaimed Fadigati. "That's quite true!"

And then he turned to the dog.

"You wretch, where have you left your babies? Aren't you ashamed of wandering round the streets at this hour? You unnatural mother!"

The dog lay down, belly to the ground, a few inches away from Fadigati's shoes.

"Beat me, kill me if you like," she seemed to be saying. "It's quite right for you to do so, and anyway, I like it!"

The doctor leant down to caress her head. The dog, with passionate devotion, refused to stop licking his hand, and even tried to reach his face with a quick stolen kiss.

"Gently, gently," Fadigati kept saying.

Followed or preceded by the dog, we continued our long walk at last. We were now approaching my home. If she went ahead of us, the dog stopped at every intersection, as if scared of losing us a second time.

"Look at her," said Fadigati, pointing. "Perhaps we ought to be like that, and be able to accept our own nature. Besides, what is one to do? Can one possibly pay such a price? There's a great deal of the beast in man: can a man give way to it? Can he admit he's an animal, only an animal?"

I burst out laughing.

"Oh no," I said. "That would be like saying: can an Italian, an Italian citizen, admit to being a Jew, only a Jew?"

He looked at me, humiliated.

"I see what you mean," he said. "Do believe me that lately I've thought of you a great deal and of your people. But, if you'll allow me to say so, if I were you. . ."

"What should I do?" I interrupted impetuously. "Accept what I am? Or rather: adapt myself to being what others want me to be?"

"I don't see why not," he answered gently. "Dear

friend, if being what you are makes you so much more human (you wouldn't be here with me, otherwise!), then why refuse it, why rebel against it? My own case is different, exactly the opposite of yours. After what happened last summer, I simply can't bear myself any longer. I can't go on; I must not. Do you believe me when I say that sometimes I can't bear to shave in front of the mirror? If only I could dress in some other way! But can you see me without this hat . . . this cloak . . . these respectable-looking spectacles? Yet on the other hand, dressed like this, I feel so ridiculous, so grotesque, so absurd! Oh no, *unde redire negant*, I really must say it! There's absolutely nothing more to be done for me, you see!"

I was silent. I thought of Deliliers and of Fadigati: one, the butcher, the other, the victim. The victim as usual forgave the butcher, consented to what he did. But as far as I was concerned Fadigati was mistaken: at that moment I was certain that I could never respond to hatred with anything but hatred.

As soon as I reached my own front door, I took the key out of my pocket and opened it. The dog put her head into the space, as if to go in.

"Get out!" I shouted. "Get away!"

The little creature ran off terrified, and took refuge by Fadigati's legs. "Good night," I said. "It's late, I really must go up."

He shook my hand with great friendliness.

"Good night. . . Keep well. . . And do give my very best wishes to your family," he kept repeating.

I left the doorway. And as he kept smiling and raising his arm in a gesture of farewell, without actually going away (sitting on the pavement, the dog too was looking up at me with a questioning air), I began to close the big door.

"Will you ring me up?" I asked him lightly, before I closed it completely.

"Well," he said, smiling a little mysteriously through the space. "We'll see."

16

He telephoned me two days later, all the same. We were at table; my mother, who was still not sitting down, answered the telephone.

"It's for you," she said, sticking her head out from the opening of the tiny room where we kept the telephone.

"Who is it?"

She came to the table shrugging her shoulder in apologetic grief at not having asked the caller's name as usual. "It's a man. . . I couldn't make out who it was."

"All you had to do was ask," I blurted out, rising. "It's not so frightfully difficult." But my heart was already pounding secretly, to warn me who it might be.

I shut myself up in the little room.

"Who is it?"

"Hello, it's me, Fadigati," he said. "I'm sorry if I disturbed you. Were you still at the table?"

I was surprised by his voice. On the telephone it sounded sharper. And his Venetian accent was more apparent.

"No, no . . . sorry, just a moment."

I opened the door that gave on to the dining-room, stuck my head through, and, without saying who it was on the telephone (I had got to the point of not even trusting my parents!) I asked my mother to cover my soup-plate with another plate. Fanny was quick to do it for her. Surprised, and immediately jealous, my father looked at me. He raised his chin as if to say: What's up? But I had already shut myself up again in the little room. "Do go on."

"Oh nothing," said Fadigati, on the other end of the line. "You told me to ring you up, and so . . . but I've disturbed you, haven't I, honestly?"

"Oh no, quite the opposite," I protested. "I'm very glad you rang. Would you like us to meet?"

I had hesitated slightly (which could certainly not have escaped him); then I went on:

"Listen, why don't you come and see us? I think Dad would be awfully pleased to see you. Would you like to?"

"No thank you . . . you really are kind . . . really and truly kind! No . . . perhaps later, it would give me the greatest joy . . . always supposing that . . . really it would make me tremendously happy!"

I was unable to think what else to say. After a rather long pause, during which the only thing I heard down the receiver was his heavy breathing, he began talking again.

"That reminds me, the dog came all the way home with me, you know."

For a minute I didn't understand.

"What dog?"

"Why, that dog the other evening . . . the unnatural mother!" he laughed.

"Oh, of course, the mongrel bitch."

"She not only came home with me," he went on, "but when we got home here, at the street door in Via Gorgadello there was absolutely nothing I could do about it, she just insisted on coming up. She was hungry, poor thing. I got a piece of salame from the pantry, some stale bread, some cheese rinds . . . you should have seen the appetite she put it all away with! But wait, I haven't finished. Afterwards, just imagine, I had to take her into my room!"

"Heavens! Right into bed!"

"Well, practically. This is how we ended up: I in bed and she on the floor in a corner. Every now and then she woke up and began whining with a tiny voice, and going to scratch the door. 'Hey, you bad dog,' I'd yell in the dark. And for a bit—quarter of an hour, half an hour—she'd be good and quiet; then she'd start up again. It really was a hellish night, I assure you!"

"But if she wanted to leave, why didn't you let her?"

"Oh I don't know: laziness. I didn't want to get up and go downstairs with her . . . you know the way it happens. As soon as it was light, in any case, I hastened to do what she wanted. I dressed and went out with her. Yes, I went out with her that time. I'd got the idea that maybe she wouldn't find her way home."

"You'd met her near the Aqueduct, if I'm not mistaken."

"Exactly. Right at the top; and in fact, at Via Garibaldi, at the corner which Via Garibaldi makes with the Spianata, I suddenly heard someone calling *Vampa!* It was a baker's boy, a dark boy on a bike. The dog flung herself on him; you can't imagine their delight. Then off they went together, he on his bike and she behind."

"Women, you see!" I said jokingly.

"Yes, I do a bit," he sighed. "She was already a long way off, almost turning into Via Piangipane, when she turned to look at me, can you believe it? Just as if to say: 'Forgive me for jilting you, kind sir, but I've just got to go away with this boy, so do be patient!' "

He laughed on his own, not at all bitterly.

"But you'll never guess why she wanted to leave during the night," he said.

"Don't tell me it was the thought of her pups that was keeping her awake!"

"Well so you *have* guessed! That was just it, the thought of her pups! D'you want a proof of it? In the corner of my bedroom where she'd slept, I later found a great pool of milk. During the night she'd had all this milk, and that was why she couldn't shut up, and kept making a fuss. Only she knows the agony she must have gone through, poor little beast!"

He went on talking: about the dog, about animals in general and their feelings, which are so like human feelings, he said, even though they may be simpler and more directly ruled by natural law. By now I was feeling pretty uneasy. Anxious not to let my parents make out whom I was talking to—as they were sitting there (no doubt about it) all ears— I answered in monosyllables. I hoped this would induce him to be brief as well. But it was no use. He looked as if he just couldn't get away from the telephone.

It was Thursday. We arranged to meet the following Saturday. He would telephone me immediately after lunch: and if the weather was fine we would take the tram and go to Pontelagoscuro to see the river Po. After the recent rains, the level of the river must have reached the danger signal. What a sight it must be!

But then at last, taking his leave:

"Good-bye, dear friend, do keep well," he repeated several times, and sounded moved. "Good luck to you and to your dear ones. . . ."

17

It rained all Saturday and all Sunday. Perhaps this was why I forgot Fadigati's promise. He didn't telephone me, and I didn't telephone him either: but, I repeat, it was sheer forgetfulness, not deliberate. It rained without stopping. Through my bedroom windows I looked at the trees in the garden: the poplar, the two elms, the chestnut, their last leaves wrenched off by the torrential rain. Only the great fir-tree in the middle, blacker and shaggier than ever, dripping strangely, seemed to enjoy the downpour.

On Sunday morning, I remember, I gave Fanny a Latin lesson. She was back at school already, but was having trouble with her grammar. She showed me a translation from Italian fairly crammed with mistakes. She just couldn't see it and I got furious.

"You idiot!" I shouted.

She burst into tears. The skin on her face, now

that the seaside sunburn had gone, was pale again, almost diaphanous, enough to show the blue veins at her temples. Her straight hair fell untidily over her heaving shoulders.

I hugged and kissed her.

"What on earth are you crying for?" I said. And I promised to take her to the cinema after lunch.

Instead I went out alone. I went to the Excelsior.

"Circle?" the cashier, who knew me, asked from high up on her chair.

She was a woman of uncertain age: dark, crimped, plump, very painted and powdered. However many years had she been there, idly ogling under her heavy eyelids like some grotesque idol? I had always seen her since the days when, as children, Mother used to send us to the cinema with the maid. We went every Wednesday afternoon, I remember, because on Thursdays there was no school; and of course we always went up into the circle.

And here was her fat white hand with its varnished nails offering me a ticket. There was something very secure, almost imperious, in the placidity of her movement.

"No, give me a seat downstairs," I said dryly, but not without having to overcome an unexpected sense of shame. And suddenly, at that moment, I remembered Fadigati.

I held out my ticket to the attendant, went inside and in spite of the crowd soon found a seat.

Throughout the film I felt strangely anxious and distracted. Several times, through the smoke and the darkness, I mistakenly thought I could make him out: with his soft hat, his cloak, his gleaming spectacles. During the intervals I looked around: in the rows of cheap seats where there were most grey-green uniforms, or in the aisles at the side, near the heavy curtains at the entrance. But it was no use, it wasn't he, he just wasn't there. Still less was he up-stairs in the circle which was crammed to the roof with youths unable to go to the football match, with smart men and girls in hats and fur coats, with army officers and police officers, with old men and middle-aged men (landowners, professional men, shop-keepers, etc.) snoozing as they waited to end the holiday first at supper, and then at their clubs. No, he certainly wasn't there. And why should he be? I asked myself, trying to be reassuring. After all, there were three other cinemas in Ferrara. And hadn't he always preferred going to the cinema after supper?

When I left, towards half-past seven, it was no longer raining. The torn, ragged clouds showed a starry sky. A warm wind had quickly dried the pavements.

I crossed the Listone and went along Via Bersaglieri del Po. On the corner of Gorgadello I glanced at his house. It was entirely closed, the lights were out. I tried to ring up from the nearby telephone box in Via Cairoli. But there was nothing, silence, no answer.

I tried again that evening from home, and the following morning again from a public box, with the same result. "He must have gone away," I told myself in the end. "When he comes back he'll obviously get in touch with me."

I was going home, walking along Via Savonarola, in the quiet of one o'clock in the afternoon. There were very few people about; from the open windows came light music from the wireless and smells of good cooking. I looked up at the perfect blue sky, against which were harshly etched the outlines of cornices and gutters. Still damp with rain, the roofs round the square of San Girolamo appeared more brown than red, almost black.

Right in front of the entrance to the maternity hospital, I ran into Cenzo, the newsvendor.

"How's the Estense getting on this year?" I asked him when I stopped to buy the newspaper. "Think we'll manage to get into B Division, Cenzo?"

Thinking I was pulling his leg, maybe, he gave me a suspicious look. He folded the newspaper, handed it to me with the change, and went away, shouting the headlines at the top of his voice.

"Bologna team badly beaten at Turin: Estense beaten at Carpiii!"

I put my key into the street door lock at home and still heard his distant voice echoing through the deserted streets.

Upstairs I found my mother radiant with happiness. My brother Ernesto had telegraphed from Paris to let us know he would be back in Italy that same evening. He would stay at Milan for half a day —tomorrow, that was. All the same he thought he'd be at Ferrara in time for supper.

"Does Dad know?" I asked her, slightly disturbed by her tears of joy, and looking down at the yellow telegram form.

"No, he went out at ten o'clock. First he had to go to the Town Hall, and then to the Bank, and the telegram arrived about midday. How thrilled he'll be! Last night he couldn't get to sleep and kept saying, If only Ernesto was at home as well!"

"Did anyone ring me up?"

"No, or rather, yes, wait a minute. . . ." Her face twisted with the effort of remembering and she looked right and then left, as if she might read the name of the person who had telephoned on the floor or the walls.

"Oh yes, Nino Bottecchiari," she said at last.

"No one else?"

"No. Nino very much wanted you to ring up. . . . Why don't you look him up sometime? He seems such a good friend."

The two of us sat down to lunch together (Fanny wasn't there; she had been asked to lunch by a school friend). My mother talked about Ernesto. She was already beginning to worry: would he take up law or medicine? Or engineering? In any case his English, which should now be perfect, would be very useful: in his work, and in his life in general.

"He'll have to keep in practice, though," I objected, just to worry her, maybe, and then with a hug to cheer her up again.

My father was later than usual that day. When he arrived we had already reached the fruit stage.

"Great news!" he exclaimed, flinging open the door.

He flung himself into his chair with an "aah" of satisfaction. He was tired and pale, but radiant.

He looked towards the kitchen door, to make sure Elisa, our cook, was not at that very moment coming in with the spaghetti; then, his blue eyes glittering with excitement, he leant across the table, obviously going to tell us all about it.

But he didn't manage to. My mother popped the unfolded telegram under his nose.

"We've got important news too," she said, and smiled proudly. "What d'you say to that?"

"Oh, it's from Ernesto," he said absently. "When's he arriving? So he's made up his mind at last."

"What d'you mean, when is he arriving?" cried my mother, hurt. "Haven't you read it, don't you see he says tomorrow evening?" She snatched the telegram from him, and, huffy as a little girl in a pet, began folding it carefully.

"You wouldn't think it was your own son!" she grumbled, looking down and putting the telegram in her apron pocket.

My father turned to me. Angrily he asked me to stick up for him and help him. But I was silent. Something stopped me interfering, and smoothing out this childish little quarrel.

"Come on, let's hear what it is," my mother agreed at last, but with the air of doing something to please me particularly.

18

This was my father's news.

Half an hour earlier, at the Bank, he had happened to meet the lawyer Geremia Tabet, who, as we knew very well, had not only been "well in" with the Fascist Party in Ferrara, but was known to enjoy the "friendship" and esteem of Bocchini, head of the police.

As they came out of the bank together, Tabet had taken my father's arm. He had recently been in Rome on business, he confided, and had taken the opportunity of "putting his nose" inside the Viminale. Given the time and circumstances, he thought His Excellency's private secretary would not even announce him. But no, the prefect, Doctor Corazza, had at once shown him into the big room where "the boss" was working.

"My dear friend!" Bocchini exclaimed at once when he saw him come in.

He got up, and came half-way across the room to meet him, shook his hand warmly, and sat him down in an armchair. After which he immediately led the conversation on to the subject of the much-aired racial laws.

"Now you just keep calm, Tabet,"—he had actually expressed himself so—"and make the greatest possible number of your co-religionists keep calm and trusting. *I'm authorized to guarantee* that racial laws will never be introduced in Italy."

The newspapers were still talking about the evils of the "Israelites", Bocchini continued; but it was only a matter of policy, a matter of foreign affairs. We must understand. These last few months the Duce had had to make the Western democracies believe that Italy was now firmly linked with Germany. What more persuasive argument could he have found than a little anti-semitism? But a counter-order from the Duce would be enough to make all the watch-dogs like Interlandi and Preziosi (the chief of police showed the greatest scorn for them) stop barking from one minute to the next.

"Well, let's hope so!" sighed my mother, who was already hanging on my father's words. "Let's hope he soon decides to give that blessed counter-order."

Then Elisa came in carrying the oval plate of

spaghetti, and my father was silent. I moved my chair, got up, and went to sit in the rush armchair by the wireless.

Why was it that I couldn't share my parents' hopes? What was it I didn't like about their enthusiasm? "Oh God, God," I said to myself, gnashing my teeth. "The minute Elisa goes out of the room I know Dad will start talking again!"

I was desperate, absolutely desperate. And not so much because I believed Bocchini had lied (after all, what the chief of police had said to Tabet might perfectly well be true) as because I saw my father so happy at once, or rather longing so much to be happy again. Well then, was this really what I couldn't bear? I asked myself. That he should be happy? That the future should smile at him again, as it had once done, *before*?

I took the newspaper out of my pocket, and glanced at the first page, then went on to the sports page right away. I tried to concentrate on the account of the football match between Juventus and Bologna that had taken place at Turin, just as Cenzo had shouted, with Bologna badly defeated. No use.

My father's joy, I thought, was like that of a child sent out of the class for a sin he had not committed, and suddenly and unexpectedly welcomed back from the empty passage into the classroom among his dear friends: not only forgiven, but recognized as not guilty and completely restored to his old position. Well, wasn't it quite right for my father to rejoice like that child? I couldn't, I just couldn't. The feeling of solitude that had been with me always these last two months was now, if anything, at this very minute, even more terrible: more complete, more definite. Well, what about it? What did I want? What did I expect?

I raised my head. Elisa was going round the table collecting the dirty plates and cutlery. The long rays of the afternoon sun pierced through the shadowy room from the room next door which opened into it. Soon, immediately after lunch, my father would go in there to have a sleep on the leather sofa. I almost felt I was seeing him there. Separate, shut in, protected, as if in a glowing pink cocoon, he slept there wrapped in his cloak, his ingenuous face turned to the light. . . .

I leant over the newspaper again.

And there at the bottom of the left-hand page, opposite the sports page, my glance fell on a fairly large headline. It said:

WELL-KNOWN PROFESSIONAL MAN FROM FERRARA
DROWNED IN RIVER PO NEAR PONTELAGOSCURO

For several seconds, I think, my heart stopped.

And yet I hadn't really understood, I still hadn't really realized.

I breathed deeply. And then I understood, yes, before I began to read the half-column under the headlines, which did not, of course, speak of suicide, but, in the style of the times, only of "misfortune". (No one was allowed to commit suicide, then: not even a dishonoured old man with no reason to stay alive. . . .)

I didn't finish reading it, anyway. I looked down. Gradually my heartbeats grew more regular. I waited for Elisa to shut the kitchen door and then, quietly, but at once:

"Doctor Fadigati is dead," I said.

GIORGIO BASSANI

Born in Bologna, Italy, in 1916, Giorgio Bassani lived in Ferrara for the first twenty-seven years of his life. After receiving a degree in literature at the University of Bologna in 1939, he became largely concerned with politics, and was one of the founders of the Action Party in 1942. The following year, he spent nearly three months in prison. The day after the fall of Mussolini, he was freed. He went to Rome, where he now lives with his wife and two children. Mr. Bassani has been an editor of the international review, *Botteghe Oscure*, since 1948, and has taught the history of the theatre at the National Academy of Dramatic Art since 1957. He is also an editor at Feltrinelli, book publishers in Milan. Mr. Bassani has written three books of verse, two previous novels, and a book of short stories.

11/15/60

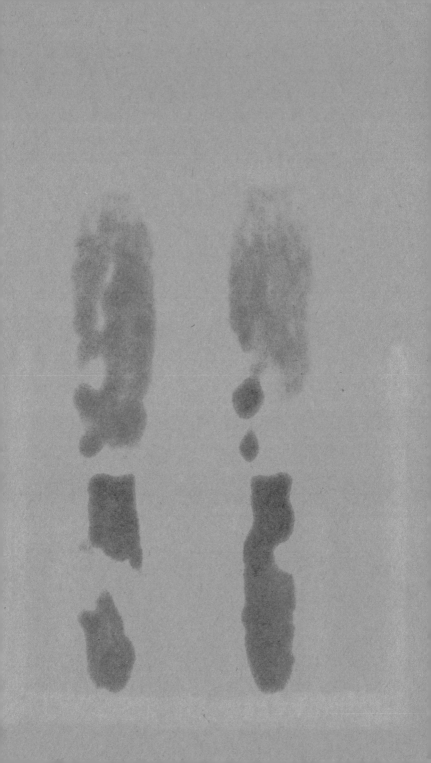